The
Lost Sister

Russel D McLean

Five Leaves Publications

www.fiveleaves.co.uk

The Lost Sister
by Russel D McLean

Published in 2009 by Five Leaves Publications
PO Box 8786, Nottingham NG1 9AW
www.fiveleaves.co.uk

ISBN: 978 1 905512 79 9

Five Leaves acknowledges financial assistance
from Arts Council England

Five Leaves is represented to the trade
by Turnaround and distributed by Central Books.
We are members of Inpress
(www.inpressbooks.co.uk)

Typesetting and design:
4 Sheets Design and Print
Printed in Great Britain

The
Lost Sister

*For Gary Smith, Robert
Macduff-Duncan, Mike Parry
and John B Dick*

*Union Street: we survived
(there really should be medals
or something)*

He doesn't waste a moment. Lets go of the axe, brings both hands round on either side of my head and slams them together. Catches me underneath both ears. The impact makes me nauseous, causes the world to go black for just a moment.

But I'm alright.

Because I don't feel anything.

And then I realise I'm on my back and suddenly it's like there are flames inside my skull.

I try to sit up. Can't do it.

Bastard's put me down for the count.

He's big. Doesn't need technique so much as momentum. He's a brawler. The kind of bastard you could see in another life slinging arseholes from pubs.

Aye, looking for zero tolerance? This is who you'd call.

I'm too stunned to even be angry.

Didn't he say it himself?

We're the same, McNee.

Meaning on the inside. Like we were kindred spirits. Some bollocks like that.

Aye, right.

But I should have seen this coming sooner. Should have known it would happen.

Of course, I've got a death wish, haven't I?

Seeking out danger. Any excuse to put myself in the path of pain.

And the way he's built…

The very embodiment.

He gives me a moment, lets me try and stand. Then kicks out with those bastard boots, knocks me back on my arse. Am I hallucinating, or do I hear a rib crack?

I'm past feeling anything. Aware of the pain, but it's like something inside me's broken and all the signals are coming in over long distance.

Do I cry out? I don't know. I could have made sound, or maybe I'm too far gone.

Jesus Christ, I don't know.

I blink, try to bring the world back in focus.

Look up at the big man.

But he's gone fuzzy. Like he's fading out of the world.

MARY FURST MISSING
24 HOURS

Chapter 1

I'd done work for Cameron Connolly before, a few covert surveillances. Some – and he's the one who made the joke – "leg" work.

He paid well, asked that I keep our dealings discreet. It was a casual arrangement. His bosses would throw a fit if he asked them to retain an investigator on the payroll.

I could have told him, "discreet" was my middle name. But we didn't play those games. He didn't want the gloss, the image, the ideals he'd grown up watching on the TV. He wanted the work.

I always delivered on that.

First time he called, he said, "I like the card."

"Aye?"

"Does the job, right? Who wants flash from a PI? Like that tosser Magnum, the one with the moustache?"

I finished it for him: "Aye, and the bright red Ferrari."

"Talk about subtle."

Connolly was on the ball. Had the gig down cold.

There's simpatico between the life of a reporter and that of an investigator. We are not the focus. When we become more important than the work – when the reporter becomes the story, or the PI becomes part of his own investigations – that's when we wind up fucking the work.

No, Thomas Magnum would never have made it in the real world.

Connolly and I had worked well together on some small cases. He was something of an arsehole, but a good reporter. Carved out his career in Edinburgh, but something happened and he took the quiet – well, quieter – life working for the *Dundee Herald.* Only got in over his head once, but once was enough. It landed him in a wheelchair.

Working an expose on Dundee's drug trade, he'd broken that cardinal rule and become part of his own story. Beaten by irate hard bastards. His spine snapped, legs left useless.

Get his wee joke now?

This happened years before I met him, of course.

He'd told me how his brother-in-law had been an investigator, too. I recognised the name, thought I'd heard something about how he'd left the business. Personal problems.

The business could eat your life.

Best if you didn't have one to start with.

***

It was a Thursday when Connolly called to ask for my help. He had a story waiting to break. "And break big," he said.

Foresight? Reporter's instinct?

Either way, he didn't know the half of it.

8

It was early afternoon, the sun was high, shining across the top of the Overgate Shopping Centre, down North Lindsay Street and streaming into the third floor window of my offices. I was drinking coffee, catching up on correspondence.

Watch the films and you might believe most PIs are walking dark alleys, snapping secret shots of illicit lovers, getting a kicking from punks and tossing off quips every time someone pulls a gun on them.

The truth?

We spend most of our days at computer screens. Farm out the specialised work to specialised individuals. When we can afford to.

And we write reports. Spend half our life trying to remember the rules of grammar we'd ignored all through school.

I'd never taken an official test, but after a few years in the business, I had a feeling my WPM could beat that of most secretarial staff.

Thing was, I wasn't typing up too many reports when Connolly called.

On the news, they talked about The Credit Crunch. Capitalise it, it's that important. Like the world was going straight to hell. Maybe so. I couldn't comment on that. But I could say that it had turned my usual pool of clients into a bunch of stingy bastards.

Guess in an economic downturn, priorities change.

So I welcomed the interruption. The chance to talk to someone else on the other end of the line. Even a hermit needs to talk every once in a while.

"It's all hush-hush," Connolly said.

I couldn't help myself. "On the QT?"

"Confidential." Connolly hesitated. I heard a door open and close somewhere nearby. He wasn't kidding about confidential if he was waiting for someone to leave. "I'm serious, pal. The coppers don't want this one getting out. Not before they say so."

"Hang on." I looked around for a pen. Found one fast, then realised I didn't have any paper. Started hunting through drawers, all the while trying my best to take in what Connolly had to say.

He said, "I should tell you up front, this isn't the usual arrangement."

"Oh?"

"The high heedjuns, they aren't exactly looking to splash the cash."

"Meaning?"

"Every penny has to be accounted for."

My services weren't on the books. Probably filed under misc, some shite like that. I'd never cared to ask. It had never mattered before.

"I don't do favours."

"You'll be compensated."

"From your pocket?"

"Ever heard of mate's rates?" He didn't sound hopeful.

I found the pen, looked at the correspondence on my email. Thought about the hours stretching ahead waiting for the next case to just fall in my lap.

Fuck it. Like I had anything better to do?

"Go ahead," I said. "I'll hear you out at least."

He dived on, like he'd never expected me to say any different. "Lead on this one's DCI Bright."

"Ernie?"

"You know him?"

"Trained under him when I went for the CID gig."

10

A gig I never completed. Couple months, waiting for the probationary period to end. After the car crash that killed Elaine, my career took what's best described as a downward spiral. Wound up with me breaking a superior officer's nose. Hardly dignified, but then life seldom is.

Things could have been worse, I suppose.

There was a notepad at the back of the bottom drawer in my desk. Couple of old numbers scribbled on the first page. I scored through them, tried to remember if they were important.

Elaine used to laugh at how disorganised I was. Couldn't figure how I got anything done.

My excuse was, I had a system, she just didn't understand it.

Her response: "Neither do you."

Aye, she'd had a point. Always did.

Connolly said, about DCI Bright, "That's it? There's something more between you and Bright. Don't kid a kidder, McNee."

Guys like Connolly could hear those things you didn't say.

"It's not important."

He let it drop. We had a surface relationship, but he understood me enough to know when I didn't want to talk about something.

"Bright's in charge, then," I said.

"Yep. Missing girl. Fourteen years old. Name's Mary Furst. Been missing since yesterday afternoon." He told me the story. Gave me the facts.

I scribbled furiously.

Reflected later.

***

Mary Furst was in her third year of high school. First year of Standard Grades.

A bright student. The kind of girl who breaks hearts, but never with malice. The kind of girl everyone likes. The kind of girl who'll never want for anything. Not an enemy in the world.

No wonder Connolly was on the case. This was the sort of story, you could tug people's heartstrings. The right details, every reader would be smudging the type with their tears.

Tragedy equals circulation.

In fairness to Connolly, he didn't seek it out, but he had this instinct. Knew when tragedy was close at hand.

This was one in the making.

Mary Furst left school at the usual time, according to the police reports. The family – just Mary and her mother these days – lived within walking distance of the Bellview Academy campus. She'd generally sling back across neighbours' gardens. That kind of neighbourhood. Most of the residents knew each other, didn't mind their kids taking shortcuts through their property as long as they behaved themselves.

Over the phone, Connolly said what I was thinking: "Thought that kind of world disappeared around 1966."

So Mary makes it home, passes Mum in the kitchen, says she's heading upstairs to get changed. Mum reminds her: homework.

So far, so domestic.

Mum pops out for milk. The shop's across the street.

Her daughter is fourteen.

Bright. Intelligent. Trustworthy. More than most

kids, if what Mum says is to believed.

But when Mum comes back with the milk...

...Mary's gone.

Chapter 2

"And why are the police hushing this up?"

Connolly chuckled like an undertaker. Amused at me, not the girl's disappearance. Journalism – like police work – brings out your cynical, callous nature. We've all got one.

He said, "I don't believe she ran off."

"Good girl or not, you get some funny ideas at that age."

"You ever go through a rebellious phase?"

I didn't answer.

Connolly persisted: "McNee, were you ever a bloody child?"

I didn't answer that, either.

"Christ, were you grown in a fucking factory?"

I broke down under the pressure. "Maybe."

"Go shite."

I couldn't resist a smile. He couldn't see me. It didn't matter. Long as I sounded like I had a poker face on. "Tell me why you don't think this one's a runaway."

"The police are acting funny. DCI Bright's a cagey bugger at the best of times, but this time he's being

14

real slippery."

Me and Ernie Bright hadn't talked in a long time. Not since I left the force. Maybe for as many personal as professional reasons.

"What's the press release say?"

"The facts. And that lovely wee postscript that asks, anything we find, could we please give it to the police and keep it under wraps."

"They're asking for help."

Connolly chuckled again. "Ah, but they're not asking for it."

"Devious bastards. That strike you as suspicious, then?"

"After a couple of years in this game, everything does."

Cynical? Aye, but he had the instincts.

I was feeling it, too. This wasn't just a missing person case. Maybe you just pick up on these things after a while. Our businesses breed paranoia.

Or maybe I just needed something to occupy my mind. Looking for a case where maybe there wasn't one. I was bored; in need of something other than the run of the mill jobs I could do in my sleep. Photographing accident sites, assisting genealogical researchers. Not the kinds of cases that got my blood boiling.

This one had potential. Might prove interesting at least.

I said, "This one doesn't go on the books."

"It's free then?"

"I'll sniff around," I said. "If it seems interesting, I come at you with a price."

"Fair enough."

It wasn't. But I guess he thought it was better than nothing.

***

The popular image of the private investigator: a pariah to the local police force.

Check the antagonism they receive in the American pulp novels. The snide remarks. The beatings. The humiliations.

Only one copper treated me like that. And DI George Lindsay had reason enough.

There were others who, most of the time, I considered friends. Like Susan Bright.

Aye; the DCI's daughter.

A Detective Constable these days. Plain Clothes. Suited her.

We met for coffee at a small Italian-style café with stone floors. Trying to mimic the continental street culture. Bringing the experience inside was the only way to do it in Dundee. The local weather was hardly suited to the task. Especially this late in the year. The frost wasn't settled yet, but it was on its way.

Listen to the weather reports on the local stations and you might expect Arctic temperatures any minute.

Half ten, the place was empty. The staff chatted at the counter, paid us no attention. Didn't matter. We were looking for private conversation, anyway. Took a tucked-away corner table near the rear, just beside the display case of desserts. Susan deliberately took the seat that faced away from them.

I said, "When'd you start drinking tea?"

Susan met that with a smile. "Coffee was keeping me up at night."

I nodded at her cup. "More caffeine in there than in mine."

"That a fact?"

"Read it somewhere."

"Give me the source."

"Give me a break."

She broke the grin; frowned. Tipped her head to the left and then the right. Trying to look at me from a different angle.

Worried me, sometimes. This way she had of seeing through my bluster. Felt a little too... intimate. Although you could chalk that up to guilt, a half-remembered night of drink and bereavement. Dangerous mixture.

"You want something?" I tried saying it with a grin. Off the cuff. Nonchalant. Not my style.

"Really, Steed," she said.

Steed. An old nickname. Got tired of explaining to people: like the actor who played Steed in the avengers. Patrick MacNee. No one ever said: *But he spelled it differently* and I'd long given up caring.

"I just thought... we hadn't talked in a while."

True enough. But not the reason I asked her out here to talk. She knew it, too. Gave me the look she'd inherited straight from her old man. The one that said, *no shite today*, and made you realise there was nothing you could hide from this woman.

The look that made her a force to be reckoned with when interrogating a suspect. Probably the look that got her the fast track to CID.

She said, "Tell me." No inflection. No stress. No implied meaning.

So I told her. Straight up. No use lying to Detective Constable Bright. Christ, but I could imagine being on the wrong side of her in an interview. She was delicate; small bones, sharp features, long fingers. And that look that said: *this is not a woman you mess with.*

She listened. Another skill every copper needs.

When I was done, she said, "You're talking about my dad's case."

I nodded.

She said, "This is what they call a conflict of interest."

I nodded again.

She ran her right hand through her hair as though pulling out the tangles. Didn't look directly at me. Said, "Remind me why I stick my neck out for you?"

I shrugged. "My rugged good looks?"

She shook her head. "Try again."

I didn't.

She said, "You're bad for my career."

"Who says that?" Like I didn't know the answer.

She had partnered with DI Lindsay for a few months after her promotion. He wasn't shy in sharing his opinions. Especially when it came to me for some reason.

Could never figure that out.

"Part of policing is politics."

Aye, the part I never liked. My attitude: just do the fucking job, forget kissing anyone's arse.

Susan's attitude, too, I guessed. But she had more sense than me. Knew when to reign back her behaviour.

She said, "I know the journalist. Connolly. Arrogant. Thinks he's… entitled." She chose that last word carefully. Maybe aware of the implications someone could pick up from it.

"Aye," I said, "he's a journalist all right. But he's not so bad."

She raised her eyebrows. "You've started seeing

the good in people?"

I almost said, "I blame you for that." Instead remained with what I hoped was a neutral expression. Said, "Did my homework. I know the coppers working the case. Didn't think they'd let father and daughter on the same gig."

"You know how it is, Steed. You remember, right?"

"Never enough people to go round." Same old story. The police were underfunded. Nothing new there. Every successive government made promises about policing and every time they fucked the boys and girls in uniform.

Not in the pleasant sense, either.

I know of one force that has a speed trap set up on a stretch of motorway notorious for speeding. But they don't have the manpower to keep a permanent eye out for naughty motorists. So they have a wooden car. I shit you not; a wooden car. painted up to look like the real thing. They erect it when there's no one available to sit sentry at police parking spots on the side of the motorway. Motorists coming down can't tell if it's real or not till they're right on top of it, and most of them aren't going to take the chance.

Creative thinking, but borne of necessity. Lack of manpower. Lack of funding. Lack of support.

The *Daily Mail* crowd bemoan the lack of powers the police have and cry bloody murder when their comfortable incomes are taxed to pay for it. Of course, you read a paper like that, you're less than half a step from hypocrisy and self-delusion in the first place.

I said to Susan, "Then this is a big case? A priority?"

"Oh, aye. Couldn't you tell when your paraplegic wee friend got interested?"

"He's not paraplegic. Not like Denzel Washington in that bloody film."

"Thought you hadn't been to the movies in decades."

"I keep up. Trailers, mostly."

"Best parts."

"What I can gather."

She smiled at me across the table. The Officer Bright façade had dropped, as it always did eventually. We spiked between two forms of communication: confrontation and… something else.

I didn't know what to call it.

"He's your client, then?"

"I'm running this down as a favour."

"What's that mean?"

"What's it sound like?"

She nodded. For a second I thought she was going to walk. Wouldn't blame her.

But she'd never walked before with all the shite I put her through. This was no exception.

Don't ask me why.

She said, "You know, part of Dad wishes you were still on the force. He'd be glad to have you working this one. Even just consulting. Christ, you were the Golden Boy."

She'd told me as much the first time we met. Back then it had sounded more like an attack, of course.

I said, "He knew me as a uniform. Nothing more."

"He's a sharp cookie."

"Like his daughter."

"Aye, well, I'm not going to deny any compliments from you."

"I'm not asking you to give me anything that's going to endanger the case," I said. "Just enough access."

"How much is *just enough*?"

How do you answer a question like that?

I said, "Tell me about her."

"Mary Furst? What do you know?"

"Good student. Well liked. Not a care in the world. At least none beyond the usual teenage angst."

"You remember how that was?"

"I can barely remember past last week."

"Somehow, I can't see you as a teenager. With the spots, the gangliness, all that good stuff."

"If anyone asks, I'll deny it."

"I'll bet you stayed out of the yearbook." She grinned, waggled her eyebrows at me.

I said, "You want to go to a casino?"

***

A couple of hours later I had photocopies of the case notes on my desk.

Unofficially, of course.

Susan still hadn't talked to her father about letting me in. Aye, who would envy her that conversation?

I skimmed the papers. The ground work had been done fast. Witness statements. Risk assessments.

Suspects.

No, scratch that last one:

Persons of interest.

Whatever you wanted to call them, it wasn't a long list.

No enemies? No one who wished her harm?

Who was this girl?

I checked what they had on her. A potted biography. Hastily assembled. They were working on deadline, here. Mary's life at school revolved around

21

drama societies, sports teams, the works. No one the police had spoken to had a bad word to say about her. Not unusual given the circumstances of her disappearance, I guess. Probably everyone was thinking about the media before the coppers opened their mouths to say word one.

That's the way the world is, now. Even the most unremarkable people are media savvy, cynical enough to know when to present their best side to the newspapers and the television.

Mary's ex-boyfriend, Richie Harrison, had been one of the first people the police talked to.

Aye, Mary had broken up with him before she disappeared, but in the report he came across as worried for her as anyone. When asked why they split he said, "It was one of those things." I could picture this teenager trying to appear mature and nonchalant, when reading between the lines I knew that he was torn up inside.

The report wrote him off. He wasn't behind it.

I was inclined to agree, but figured I had to speak to the lad myself. People are more than words on a page. Sometimes even the clearest reports can leave out the subtlest of details.

All the same, reading the report, I was thinking, Jesus, when you can split with a teenage boy and he shrugs it off like a rational human being... you're truly something special.

The school and Mary's social life had been the investigation's primary area of focus. Not that the police found much of anything except a whole lot of concerned friends.

When they looked to her family, of course, things got interesting.

They say you can choose your friends but not your family.

Truer words never spoken.

It wasn't her immediate family that caught my attention of course.

But you'd never choose to have a man like David Burns as your uncle. No matter how many times removed. And godfather? Your moral guardian and role model? Aye, forget that one.

Chapter 3

When I called Susan back, I asked her if she was sure they had the family connections right.

"Oh, aye. Dad's heading round to talk to the old git this afternoon. See what he knows." She hesitated. I could sense her gearing up to ask a question I'd been trying to avoid myself. "Given your... history with Burns, do you really want to touch this case?"

I didn't say a word.

Thinking about David Burns.

The old git.

Old bastard, more like.

***

It's hard to open the local papers and not see a mention of the man. He's a local hero. Dundee Boy made good, as so many people say. Has interests in the local community, does what he can, publicly, to be seen attempting to rejuvenate the poorer areas, keeping the profile of the city high and proud.

A local hero. A good man.

A scumbag.

All that charity, that social work, those exhaustive public appearances are just so much smoke. He knows how to play the game, act untouchable. Except he's knuckle deep in drug money, extortion rackets, underground deals, blackmail. You name it, he's behind it. The kind of man who's unafraid to employ violent methods as a means to an end. Long as he doesn't have to get involved himself. Oh, no. He's got an image to maintain. And, aye, he'd say himself he has limits. Never anything with children. Never in his street. Call that his moral yardstick.

A year earlier, I'd got myself involved with his affairs. Almost lost my life because of it. Came out with a broken hand and a good friend lying close to death in the hospital.

Swore I'd never go near Burns again.

Or else I'd crucify him the first chance I got.

I'd called him the devil incarnate. And worse. Hard to believe he was related – however distantly – to Mary Furst. The saintly girl I'd been reading about in the police reports.

But there it was: this missing girl, no matter how smart and sweet she was… she had a dangerous kind of family.

And maybe that put a whole new spin on her disappearance.

***

"What do you figure?" I asked Susan. "Turf war?"

Susan seemed to think about it. "You mean Gordon Egg? We've been talking to boys in the Met. Those flames have been extinguished."

"You really believe that? Last I knew, Egg had a price on our man's head."

"Call it an uneasy truce between London and Dundee, then. Whatever, this has nothing to do with Burns's... private business."

Some euphemism.

I paced my office to the windows. Outside, the skies were dark, the clouds hanging heavy.

"It's not too late for you to back out, Steed," Susan said. "Connolly would understand."

I made this non-committal sound. As in: I'd consider it. My track record for listening to good advice was spotty at best. And worse when it came to listening to Susan. She knew that as well as I did, didn't push any further. She'd said her piece; what more could she do?

Susan said, "You want to ask questions, you want to tag along, you talk to Dad."

I took a breath. One of those prices I wasn't sure I could pay.

Still thinking: *David Burns.*

***

I told Susan I had things to do. Remained deliberately unclear on whether I wanted to remain on board with the Furst case.

I hung up the phone. My chest started to constrict, like someone had wrapped an iron band around it and the metal was shrinking fast. I fought to control my breathing. Feeling dizzy, a little nauseous. My mind moving fast, replaying my conversation with Susan.

Concentrate on the moment. The job. The case.

But other memories intruded. Like my life had

disconnected itself. A tape winding back on itself; becoming twisted like a nest of serpents.

I remembered:

Soft skin beneath my lips, the scent of perfume knocking my brain out of my skull.

The agony as someone stamped their foot down hard on my fingers on a rain soaked evening.

My hands seized up, muscles contracting, blood rushing away from my extremities. I knew what was happening, had to fight to control it.

I fell back against my desk, just about toppled right over the top. Steadied myself. Concentrated on staying upright.

On the rhythm of my breathing.

Everything else was just a distraction.

Concentrate on the breathing.

Attacks like these used to come on and off during my teenage years. They lingered, recurring once or twice since my mid-twenties. But never anything quite like this. Easy to pass them off as growing pains over a decade earlier. But now... could I dismiss them?

Maybe there was a reason. A psychological tick that sent my body into some hellish fight-or-flight parody without warning. But I figured it wasn't anything I wanted to explore. Not yet, anyway.

Chapter 4

DCI Ernie Bright got out from behind his desk when I knocked at the door. He moved slowly. Old age, maybe. I didn't want to think about it.

The desk itself was cluttered. Paperwork spread out. Family photos, most of them old, featuring a Susan young enough you had to wonder if the newly minted Detective Constable wasn't embarrassed to walk in here.

Then again, maybe that was the idea.

Ernie gave me the courtesy smile, but I couldn't read what was going on in his head. Maybe I was distracted by how much he'd aged. Or else he was just that good.

It had only been a couple of years since we last spoke, but Ernie looked more like ten had passed. His hair – salt and pepper before – had turned a distinguished silver and was longer; swept back from the temples. It gave him a distinguished air. Aristocratic seemed a good word to describe the way he looked now. His face was thinner than I remembered, too, and the lines cut deep into his weathered skin. The eyes were sunk deep, too, but still flashed with the energy of a much younger man.

He said to me, "You're looking older."

I hadn't considered how much I might have changed.

Ernie gestured for me to sit down. "I'm going to guess at something, Ja – uh, I mean McNee." Remembering how I didn't like people to use my first name. I used to kid that I even made my parents call me McNee. No one's ever been sure how serious I am on that point. And Mum and Dad aren't around any more to ask. Ernie was grinning at me, like he'd made the slip on purpose. Wanting to see if I was still the same man he had known.

In some ways, I hoped not.

"You were always good with wild guesses," I said. "Hunches, too."

He snorted, put his hands behind his head as he leaned back in the swivel chair. "If I don't give you access, you're going to poke around anyway." Not a question.

I couldn't say anything in response. Opted for a half-shrug.

He said, "You were a tenacious little prick even as a constable. One of the things I liked about you." An accusation?

Fuck him if it was. He wasn't my superior any more. Nothing he could do to me that hadn't been done. So why was I still on the defensive?

"The same can't be said for others."

He got it. "Lindsay's not attached to this case. Oh, I know he'd be all over it. You know how he is since he had his wee lad, but a case like this requires someone with a... subtle touch."

Subtlety wasn't one of Lindsay's traits. A lot of

people in the department talked about how he got results, as though that one simple fact somehow excused the fact he was an unreconstructed arsehole.

In the police, results wash away all other sins.

I pressed on: "How much access do I get?"

Was he happy that I'd avoided airing my opinions on Lindsay? Did I see a smile play about the DCI's usually tight lips? Christ, time was I might have been able to tell. He had been my self-appointed mentor and now... now we were strangers. Alien to each other in the worst possible ways. He said, "How much do you want?"

"Much as I can. All the way. I need to know when there's a break. What the break is. What it means. I need to be there in meetings, observing interviews, all that good stuff."

"You're asking a lot for a courtesy."

I gave it a shrug. Emphasis; making sure he got the point. "Like you said, I'm a tenacious prick."

"Jesus, what is it with you? You're bored, don't have anything else to do?" He shook his head, leaned forward. "When I tell you to back off, you do it. Don't think I don't know about you and David Burns. I don't want this getting personal. There's a girl's life at stake. So when I say... that's the condition."

I hesitated long enough to worry him. Then I said, "That's the condition." Shot him a smile, too. Playing with him just a little.

***

First time I met Ernie Bright, he called me up to give evidence on an internal police matter. A DI by the name of Griggs had got himself in hot water over his handling of a murder case. I'd been present at the scene when Griggs had taken charge. Didn't do much more than guard the door at the crime scene. Standing around the hall of a halfway house keeping away the lookie-lous and the gawpers who came out to see what was going on.

All of them wondering, who finally got killed. And was it by their own hand or someone else's?

It has been a shitty detail, but I followed the chain of command in those days. And why not? One of these days, I figured I'd be the one asking some poor sod to do the dirty work. The copper's version of karma.

I remember waiting to go in for the interview, sitting on a felt-covered chair in the hall outside and sweating beneath my uniform. Not knowing what to do. Whether there was a right or wrong way to approach this.

I'd picked up fast on the politics of policing. As with every other job, there were ways of approaching affairs that had little to do with the work and everything to do with saying the right things to the right people.

When the Chief Constable poked his head out and asked me to come in, I wasn't even sure I could stand. In those days I was always waiting to be found out as some kind of fraud. As much as I loved and respected the Job, I always worried that maybe I wasn't right for it. Or it wasn't right for me.

When I walked in, I saw three men behind the desk. The Chief, imperious. The air of Ming the Merciless about him. Minus the dodgy facial hair. And he was shorter, fatter than the Emperor of

31

Mongo. Of course, it was all in the eyes. Attitude is what people remember about you.

On the other side of the Chief sat two men in uniform. One was DCI Black; a grumpy bastard, originally from Lothian. Griped constantly about Dundee. Kept going on about how much cleaner Edinburgh was. How much more beautiful. Christ, even if it wasn't true, I had the feeling he'd find some way to justify his hatred of the city; Dundee has a polarising effect on those who come from the outside.

The other copper present was Ernie Bright. In those days I only knew him by sight and reputation. He had a good reputation. The word, *fair* was used. Along with, *a good man*. Aye, try throwing a brick in a room full of senior officers and see if you hit many of those.

The meeting went as well as could be expected. I didn't know anything, they tried to make out like maybe I did. I kept to my line, they finally let me go.

When I was walking down the hall, I heard footsteps behind me, turned and saw Ernie Bright following me. I stopped, let him catch up. He leaned close, and said in a voice close to whisper: "You ever want to transfer to CID, let me know."

Anyone asks what I did in there to impress him, their guess is as good as mine.

***

Do I ever regret it? Leaving the force?

Aye, of course I do.

But there are a lot of things I regret. Some of them are stupid. Others make me want to get hit by lightning. But isn't everyone the same?

32

We all have our ways of dealing. Time was I'd have hashed things out with Elaine. My sounding board. No idea how she put up with the rants, my disjointed monologues and irrational annoyances. Ask me why she loved me and I couldn't say. I'm just glad she did.

When she died, I couldn't go to her graveside. Afraid of how it might affect me. To break down like I feared was a sign of weakness that Scottish men are taught to dismiss.

We don't break down. We don't cry.

At least, that was the excuse I used for myself.

What I held on to for the longest time was the anger. Finding it hard to let go.

But after a while, I came to accept her death. And the anger that came with it. Started making regular visits to the cemetery. Feeling like maybe I should talk, but not wanting to be one of those lunatics mumbling to themselves in the graveyard. They say it's perfectly healthy; I say it's just an embarrassment.

Didn't stop me wanting to say things, though.

The grave is simple, erected by her family. I didn't have much say in the matter. There's an inscription in French on the headstone. I don't speak the language so well, but her sister told me what it meant:

Our nature consists in movement. Absolute rest is death.

Maybe if I'd known that earlier, a lot of things would have been brought into perspective.

It was late afternoon when I stood in front of the stone, read the inscription even though I could quote it without hesitation.

I closed my eyes, tried to remember her face. Little by little, she was escaping me. Getting so I could only remember how she looked when I came across old photographs.

Some days, I thought I was betraying her by starting to heal.

Overhead, heavy skies threatened. The grass at my feet was stiff, with a thin covering of frost that sparkled gently in the late afternoon light. I could feel it crush when I pressed my weight down on the ground. Wind rattled at the branches of old trees that stood in the grounds of the Balgay cemetery, and I felt a strange sense of loneliness. I was the one living person in a field of the dead.

I crouched in front of the headstone, traced the dates that marked Elaine's life with my index finger. Closed my eyes.

Tried to conjure up her face.

Wished she was here with me. To answer my questions. Offer reassurance. Remind me what it was to be in love with life again.

Here was the reality: she wasn't coming back.

I was alone.

In the end, that was the one inescapable truth of my life.

Maybe I was alive. Had moved to a place of understanding, after all.

***

In the car, I read through the files again. Looking for something I had missed. Drinking in the details.

Working it like a real case and not just a favour for a friend.

I was parked near the cemetery gates; had turned the interior lights of the car on as the day darkened considerably. Grey light made it hard to see, and I was grateful for the shelter as rain started to whip down over the car. The winds got up enough that I could feel a gentle rocking motion.

Reading the files I kept coming back to one name: Burns.

Susan had told me she didn't suspect the disappearance had anything to do with Mary's Godfather's more unsavoury connections. Can't say that I was so sure.

The thing I had to figure, why was I drawn to this case? It wasn't about doing Connolly a favour.

And could I say that the girl's disappearance affected me that much? Maybe reminded me of someone I used to know. Some girl at school, perhaps.

Or was I looking for some closure with Burns? Some way of taking revenge by tying him into the girl's disappearance. By making him the bad guy. By exposing the bastard once and for all.

Was I looking to make this my case for all the wrong reasons?

Chapter 5

The Neighbourhood Watch had been out in force. Every lamppost had a laminated poster stuck on it. Colour picture: head and shoulders of Mary smiling coyly at the camera. Not really wanting her picture taken, but knowing it was going to happen anyway.

When I parked the car outside the Furst house, I stopped to look at one of the fliers – a pixellated printout – and felt something that might have been longing or sadness. Possibly both. A longing for something I could never have had and a sadness that even if Mary were to return, she would never again be that girl in the picture.

It's funny how pictures can affect us that way. Light and angle and expression give us these impressions. Snapshots make us think we know a whole person.

But I didn't know this girl.

Maybe never would.

I turned away, opened the front gate of her mother's house, walked up to the door, knocked fast. Too late to double back.

No choice, then, but to wait.

After a while, if only to keep myself standing there, I knocked again.

The door opened. A woman slipped her head out, nervous, not sure what to expect. In her late thirties, but her daughter's disappearance had added years. Her hair was flat and lifeless, her skin smooth but dull, and her eyes seemed heavy with the kind of knowledge no one should ever have. She might have been attractive if it wasn't for the fact she appeared so close to death; a look in her eyes as though she wished she could feel that bony hand upon her shoulder.

Jennifer Furst. Mary's mother.

She wasn't past thirty-five. Looked so damn tired. I introduced myself.

People joke a lot about the "foot in the door" methods employed by door to door salesmen. Truth of the matter is, putting your foot in the door doesn't really change anyone's mind, although it usually does result in bruising or broken bones. A guy I knew used to be a salesman, said he had a real method of getting sales; figuring who were the chumps and who the timewasters. It worked pretty well, I found. Not just for salesmen.

As I gave my name, I took my hand out my coat pocket as though to offer it, dropped the pen that had been in there.

The pen rolled.

Jennifer Furst bent down to pick it up.

My friend had called this action, "The calling card of the sucker."

I was better disposed. Figured I learned a lot about Mrs Furst from that one gesture.

She may have been related to David Burns by blood, but she was not him. I didn't know whether to

37

feel glad for that or guilty at using her misery to satisfy my own curiosity.

***

We moved to the living room. Jennifer Furst gestured for me to take a seat on the sofa, flopped herself into a large armchair which seemed too imposing for a woman of her stature.

The room itself was neat; no real clutter. And – this was what struck me – no pictures on the wall, although the fireplace held a few photos in frames. Many of them of Mary herself. You could chart her whole life, from gurning little girl to smiling teenager.

Call that heartbreaking. There was still that nagging sensation that maybe she reminded me of some girl I used to know. Or I simply wished that she did.

The sofa had its back to the window, faced the rear wall of the room. Jennifer Furst's chair was in a corner, again giving this impression that it was a place she could hide away.

She said, "I'd offer you tea, but I don't want to give you an excuse for staying."

I didn't sense hostility so much as a tentative grasp, the hope that here sat someone who could help her.

Aye, check the romantic in me.

"I'll level with you, Mrs Furst. I'm working with a reporter." I bulldozed on before she could tell me to get out. "But the more I learn about your daughter, the more I just want her back alive. I used to be a copper, and I'll tell you that the officers working your case are –"

"Not going to find my daughter."

No defence there. What can you say to that? Especially delivered in such calmly considered tones?

"They're not going to find her," she said. "Unless she wants to be found."

"You think she ran away?"

Mrs Furst seemed ready to say something, but shied from it at the last moment. She tucked her legs up underneath her, and turned her head to the side.

I said, "It's better than the alternative."

She nodded, and I felt this pain in my chest, like my heart wanted to give out. Realised too late what I'd said to her, and recognised the pain as guilt.

I wanted to leave. Stand up, walk out the room, maybe even pretend I'd never been there in the first place.

And I had to ask myself the same question I felt sure Mrs Furst was dancing around: what was I doing there?

But instead she asked, "Are you working with the police?"

I figured it was the same question rephrased. And I sidestepped it: "Observing the investigation."

"Why?"

"I want to see your daughter safe."

"There's more than that."

Maybe.

We were on the second floor landing. The door in front of us was shut. The tag two thirds of the way up read *Mary's room* and looked old, as though it had been there for all of her fourteen years.

A marker of childhood. Even as a teenager, you hold onto that innocence of childhood as long as you can. Privately, sometimes, as you assert your own identity. The truth is that growing up frightens you.

So in your own space, there are reminders of what it is to be young. Talismans and keepsakes. Memories.

Something about this case was pulling me in. Not simply that I'd been asked to look into it. More than that…

I looked at the door again.

The name.

I turned back to Mrs Furst. "I told you I was working with a reporter. But on some level… I need to know that your daughter will be returned, Mrs Furst. The deeper I look into this, the more I see a person at the heart and not… not a news story or –"

"Really, what do you know about her?"

Nothing.

"Enough. Enough to know that you want her home."

She looked suspicious.

"Working with a reporter," she said, as though thinking it over. "I can't stop them writing about her. But maybe they can… maybe they can do it right. Maybe you can tell your friend the truth, aye? About my girl."

I nodded. "I have questions."

"She was never in any trouble."

"I don't doubt it."

"I loved her."

I looked back at the door again. At the sign. Said, "This was her world, behind the door."

"What are you looking for?"

I answered fast. "Mary," I said. "That's all. I'm just looking for Mary."

Chapter 6

Mary Furst's room seemed untouched.

Her mother did not come inside with me. She stayed out in the corridor, acting as though the door was still closed to her.

She said, "After the police were done, I made it back the way it had been." She hesitated before adding, "In case… she comes back."

What do you say to that?

I opted for silence, stood in the middle of Mary's room and looked around. The bed was made by a mother's hand. Sheets tucked tight, pillows fluffed and inviting. A few stray stuffed animals at the head of the bed; inanimate pets. Probably closer to Mary than some of the friends she had at school.

Like I said: talismans… reminders… memories.

There were pictures on the wall. The framed ones were paintings. Originals, not prints. Looked like they'd been given as gifts. A recurrent theme of dogs made me guess at a lost family pet. Not recent, but Mary had been old enough to be struck by the loss.

Other images were more expected: torn posters of bands and films. Guys – tanned, with white teeth – glared down, with open shirts, one or two dispensing with them altogether. How much of a fight had that caused with Mum?

I checked the bookshelves. Waist high along one wall, the top shelves were decorated with knick-knacks; pewter dragons with false gems for eyes, some cute looking models, a couple of pictures of other kids I guessed were her friends, all framed perfectly. Looking at the books themselves: a few old children's classics – battered and well read – sat alongside more adult works. I smiled when I saw *Catcher in the Rye*, and noticed the crack in the spine. The kind of book, you get to it at the right age, I hear it can change the way you look at things. Come to it older, as I did, you wonder what all the fuss was about. I pulled the copy, thumbed.

An inscription:
Will this change your life, too?
Love,
D.

Feminine handwriting. The attention to detail you don't get with most boys. I popped the book back into place. Didn't figure it as too important, but maybe teenage angst had played some role in this particular drama.

Also on the shelves, of course, there were the obligatory *Harry Potter* novels. The older ones were cracked and thumbed, the newer ones looking fresher with the latest edition hardly looking touched. Lost interest? Or an appreciation of how much the books were going to be worth in their new condition?

More space was given to CDs. Music from bands I

didn't know. *Maximo Park, Biffy Clyro*. The names meant nothing to me.

The computer was tucked away in a corner. I didn't figure her for a geek, but I guessed she knew her way around the machine. I turned back to Mrs Furst, gestured to the computer, still feeling like an intruder.

She said, "Aye, if you must."

I booted the PC. No password protection. As though asking an idle question, I said, "You have your own computer?"

"No. I can barely turn the bloody thing on."

That meant no password because there was no *need* for a password. Mary felt safe enough with her mother booting up the machine because the woman wasn't about to go snooping. Maybe not because she didn't want to, but more because she just couldn't.

I turned away from Mrs Furst and mouthed the words, *Sorry*, as though Mary could actually see me or at least sense what I was doing.

The computer whirred, slow. Not out of date, but getting there. I checked the modem, saw the *PC Activity* light start flashing as *Windows* kicked in. The start up sound boomed at me, "Come with us now, on a journey through time and space..." The desktop was decorated with an image of two cats in a basket; stupefyingly cute.

I checked the documents folder first.

Lot of schoolwork by the looks of things. Essays and projects. Saved pages from the internet. Adobe documents. Lots of scanned images.

I checked Outlook Express. Bypassing the password got me into her saved emails. She wasn't *that* security conscious. Organised meticulously.

I clicked through folders, named for recipients.

Most of her friends identified by nickname.

I skimmed e-mails. Checking for keywords: anything that signified tension or worry. Nothing jumped out. The usual back and forth: worries about schoolwork, boys, parents.

Check the local folders, skim past the number of messages in each folder. Check the disparities.

One name:

Deb.

362 messages. More than double any other number.

I figured Deb for the mysterious "D" who'd gifted Mary *Catcher.* Clicked through a couple of the mails. Shorthand, mostly. Never specific. A lot of talk about classes and how Mary shouldn't be afraid to nurture her talent.

Read more like a concerned older relative than anything.

Maybe something more. Or was I looking for connections where there were none?

I searched for messages from her last known boyfriend, Richie Harisson. Finally found him in the folder marked:

Ra-Ra-Rasputin

An in joke?

Aye, you're full of them as teenagers. Like a secret code; a way of hiding what you're thinking from the rest of the world.

Chapter 7

Downstairs, in the living room, I drank coffee, sitting across from Jennifer Furst. The coffee was instant. She'd put the milk in without asking. I didn't complain.

"Did you ever argue with your daughter?"

"I loved her."

"Doesn't mean you didn't fight," I said. "I've never been a parent, but I know I used to fight with mine when the mood took."

She smiled, hung her head. For a moment, she didn't look so tired. As though the idea of her daughter had taken away a few years. She said, "The last year we fought about church."

"Church?"

"We go every Sunday. Always have done. She used to do well in Sunday School, too, you know. When she got older, we had a wee talk about it and she stopped that part. But I told her she had to keep going to Church. It's what our family always did."

"You're Catholic."

She nodded. "I had David... her godfather try and –"

"David Burns?"

She hesitated. "I know what you're thinking." She sat back in her chair. Disconnected again. She'd seen something in my face.

I needed to play more poker.

"You were a copper, aye? You said that when you came in?"

"A long time ago."

"I know what you people think of David. I know who he's been. The things he's done. But he's family." Jennifer's Great-Uncle, but they were clearly close. Why else would he be Mary's godfather?

"He loves your daughter."

"Treats her like his own."

I couldn't imagine it. Burns always talked up his family man image, but knowing what I did about him the claim had never sat true with me.

"He made her keep going to Church?"

She nodded.

I wanted to laugh. Remembered the story about Burns, back when he was making his name and collecting debt for one of his predecessors, how he nailed an insolvent priest to the cross in his own church.

This time, she didn't see anything in my face.

"I guess she got moody lately. Like all teenagers. It's strange, you know, to see them turn into a real person. Some days, I think I don't know her at all."

"Has she run off before?"

Jennifer Furst shook her head.

"Some days, I was beginning to think I didn't know her at all," she said again.

"Like she wasn't your daughter?"

She flinched at that. And who could blame her?

"I didn't mean it like that," I said, trying awkwardly to cover my mistake. "When kids grow up, turn into adults, it can be like we just don't know them any more." I didn't sound convincing.

But she seemed to calm down. Adjusted her position, sat facing me again. "I guess it was like that," she said. "I didn't understand who she was. What she wanted from life." She licked her lips; a nervous gesture. Didn't seem to be talking to me any more. Carrying on an internal conversation I got the feeling she'd been avoiding for a long time. "The last few years, it's like she's been looking for herself. It's something I can't help her with. I don't know if anyone can."

***

In the back garden, on the mobile.

Susan answered fast.

"One thing."

I could hear her draw breath. Get ready to snap at me.

I got in first:

"Tell me who Deborah is."

"What?"

"Deborah. Name on Mary's computer. More emails than anyone else put together. Doesn't read like she's one of her school friends. I mean, she reads older. Not the kind of emails a teenage girl would send. I know someone's got to have been through the mail, and unless they were a bloody eejit, they'll have seen the same things that –"

"Where are you?"

She already knew. I'd given the game away. "If I tell you that, I don't think you'll be happy."

"Do I sound happy now?"

Honestly, I wasn't sure. This kind of sparring, we seemed to excel at it. A wee game we played.

Of course, games are meant to be fun.

"Do you know the name?"

She relented. I could picture her rolling back her eyes. "I know the name. Deborah's Mary's art teacher."

"Aye?"

"When we talked to Richie Harrison, Deborah's name came up. The two of them got close. Mary and Deborah, I mean. Richie doesn't say it, but he blames Deborah for Mary breaking up with him."

"What's that supposed to mean?" I had to wonder if I was picking up on innuendo where none existed.

"At this point in time, Steed, close means close and nothing else. We don't know the context. We have a pissed off schoolboy telling us how teacher stole his girl away."

"As in…?"

"As in Mary spent more time around Deborah than Richie. Doesn't mean anything."

"Or it means everything."

"Thought you were hands off." I could sense her taking a breath on the other end of the line, deciding if she really wanted to ask the next question.

"What are you doing at the girl's house?"

"You have an address for Richie Harisson?"

"I went over this. And so did my dad. You're observation *only*."

If she'd been there I might have tried for a cute grin. *Who, me?* Probably failed as well. All the same.

"I'm not looking to tread on anyone's toes. Just to help. Maybe if I have a wee chat… I'm not a copper. You know, people get nervous around –"

"This is how these things start."

"I'm looking to help. I won't do anything without consulting you or your dad."

"Remember the last time you promised to back out?"

I should have expected that. How could I forget? I'd wound up with a friend almost dying from a bullet wound to the belly, three dead bodies on my conscience and two psychotic bastards trying to kill me and nearly succeeding.

"I'm a different person, now." Did it sound convincing? I wasn't sure.

"Things are different?"

"You know they are."

She hesitated. Then gave me an address to the west of the city. Said, "We never talked."

I'd guessed at that, already.

Chapter 8

Someone was waiting beside my car. Dark tracksuit trousers, white t-shirt, he had muscles on display and wanted the world to look at them. His hair was cut short, swept forward and held down with gel. His eyebrows grew close together, nearly touching above his nose. He smoked with the practised air of someone who doesn't even think about what he's doing any more.

"Help you?" I asked as I came out of the front gate.

He grinned, flicked away the cigarette. In the half-light of early evening, the orange sparks drew attention as they exploded into the air.

"McNee?"

"Can I help you?" Maybe he didn't hear me the first time.

He cocked his head to one side, folded his arms across his chest. Intimidation? Maybe, but I wasn't about to fall for it. I'd been threatened by worse. Or better. Depending how you looked at it.

He said, "Mr Burns wants a word."

I shook my head, made to push past him, get into

the car. "I've got nothing to say to him."

The lug put a hand on my shoulder as I opened the door, pulled me back. "Aye, he said you wouldn't want to come. It'll be worth your while, pal."

Pal. The magic word that made everything all right.

"I doubt it."

"He also said, if you didn't come, he'd make sure the police found out a few things you'd rather they didn't know."

I straightened.

"About a gun you... *found*... last year. One you used in self-defence."

The gun that had been given to me by Burns himself. If he came forward about *that*, he was putting himself in hot water as much as me.

All the same... this told me he was serious.

***

I followed the other guy's car, a beat up Ford 206, looked like it had been through the wars.

I didn't need to keep too close. Knew where I was going.

Burns wanted to meet at his house. This was the only reason I agreed to go along.

If we were meeting at his house, it meant nothing would happen to me. No extra-legal offers would be made. At least... not explicitly.

The drive took maybe fifteen minutes. We'd missed the rush hour traffic in the city centre by a few hours. Try and go anywhere in Dundee around five in the evening and you'd better not be in a hurry.

Burns's house was a modest, two-storey affair. He

could have afforded a bigger place, but this house had meaning for him. It was the first home he had bought; he had raised his family here.

Burns thought of himself as a family man.

An impression that Jennifer Furst had tried to reinforce during our talk.

Just don't think of all the sons and daughters and mothers and fathers he destroyed with his drug trade. Oh, no, they didn't count. No, he was a family man but only where *his* family were concerned.

The man himself stood outside the front door, dressed in a heavy dressing gown and slippers, puffing away at a cigarette. He smiled when he saw my car pull up and walked down to the front gate to greet us. I noticed a limp. But other than that, he was standing strong. His back straight. His eyes unfaltering. Watching me as I came through the gate and walked towards him.

Last time I'd seen him, he'd been in a hospital bed. His hard man act gone, his body screaming frailty. How much of this apparent recovery was an act? A man like Burns had to be all front. No weakness. The life he chose.

"Mr McNee," he said. "A pleasure to see you again. It's been a long time. You don't call. And here I thought we were friends." He grinned, amused with his own humour.

I didn't grin. Didn't say anything.

"You're a coffee drinker, right? Come inside."

My newfound friend was still in his car, parked a few metres up the road. I turned around to look at him, saw he was still behind the wheel. He threw me a wink, and edged the car out of the space he'd parked in.

Burns ran a tight ship.

His lads learned the value of discretion. Knew when to make themselves scarce.

***

The kitchen was as I remembered: glistening and relatively unused. A showpiece.

I took a seat at the breakfast bar without being invited. Playing up the fake vibe he was trying to give. We were old friends. There was no bad blood between us.

Aye, right.

The coffee bubbled away in a percolator. Burns poured two cups, brought them over. "No milk, aye?"

I resisted the urge to tell him to go fuck himself.

Instead, I accepted the cup.

Burns said, "A good, *honest*, businessman needs to train his brain to remember things. The smallest details matter when dealing with people, aye? Not that this mattered last time you were here." He fixed me with what I guessed was supposed to be a friendly smile. "I was out of milk, anyway. Details, son, details. Forget someone's name for a moment and months of carefully built trust can slip down the drain. You understand that, right?"

"Aye. There's a lot of things I never forget."

He smiled at that, chuckled and raised his mug to his lips. He sipped, placed it back down on the breakfast bar. I noticed he hadn't sat down.

I said, "You're looking well."

"What doesn't kill us only makes us stronger, right? Your granny say that as well?"

"Never knew my gran."

"Pity. Family is important. I am a family man. Built my business so I could provide for them."

"Aye, and they all love you for it."

A deliberate jab, if clumsy. Burns's son was an accountant, moved to Edinburgh to escape his father once he was old enough to realise just exactly what it was dad really did for a living. The two never talked. I wondered if Burns knew anything about the lad's life.

But other than a momentary twitch, there was nothing to gauge Burn's reaction to my blunt attack.

"You know that Mary Furst was family to me. My niece. Twice removed, but all the same... and she is my goddaughter."

"I never pictured you as the religious type."

"Every Sunday, McNee, without fail."

I wondered if he went to the Confessional. If so, what he talked to the Father about in there. What crimes did he admit to when he thought there was no one else around except the priest and the Lord Almighty?

What lies does a man like Burns tell his God?

He said, "She's a good girl. I'm serious. So smart, she makes me proud." He left the kitchen, moving swiftly and with purpose. I noticed he was still talking about her in the present tense. He believed she was still alive.

Some people, knowing the things that he knew, might have already given up hope.

I stayed where I was, breathed in the scent of the coffee he'd handed me and waited.

He came back with a framed painting. A portrait of himself in oils. I figured from the slightly darker hair that it was a couple of years old.

"She was thirteen when she painted that," he said. "Gave it to me on my birthday." He was smiling. For a moment I could have believed he was a human being; that he could genuinely care for another person.

But I shook it off.

It was a delusion. Had to be. This man manipulated people every day. I couldn't afford to believe anything he told me.

"I'm observing the official police investigation," I said. "Eyes and ears only."

"For personal reasons?"

"I can't disclose that information."

"Client privilege?"

I nodded. Figured it would keep him off my back if he thought that.

"And yet you told Jennifer Furst about the reporter?"

He must have seen the wince. I couldn't stop it. Not when I realised how Burns had figured my involvement. He wasn't simply keeping an eye on the Furst house. Jennifer Furst had called ahead first chance she got. Told him everything about my little visit.

Did I believe it could have gone down any other way?

"Whatever you want," I said, "I'm hands off in this investigation."

"I know what you think of me," he said. "But I love that girl. I want to find whoever took her. I want her back at her mother's. I want another portrait drawn of me before I get too fucking old."

Burns sipped at his coffee again.

Mine still sat untouched on the breakfast bar. Cooling.

"Last time we met, McNee, I said that I knew you. That we were more alike than you care to admit. I don't say anything I don't mean. Don't believe anything I don't think I can prove."

"I proved you wrong."

He smiled. Patiently. Indulgently. I wanted to punch him. "We share the same worry over Mary. My fears of course are personal. She's my goddaughter. Might as well be my own daughter. I care for her like that. You... I don't know why you're so worried about her."

"Empathy," I said. "Doesn't matter if she's related. Right there, that's the difference between us."

He smiled. "Your years as a copper... they drill that hate right into you, don't they? They say about men like me, these are the bad men and they are evil. The bad men, your superiors say, are not like us. They are not like the man on the street. They are not like the *victims*. They can never be victims."

"Would you call yourself a victim?"

He turned, took his mug to the stainless steel sink and poured away what remained of his coffee. Couldn't be cold yet.

"A survivor," he said.

He seemed tense, shoulders bunched, and every movement controlled. Keeping his back to me, too. I remembered how he'd been in the hospital. At the time, I'd thought maybe I was the first person in years to see him truly afraid.

He'd shown me something he never intended. Something no one else had seen. Maybe that was what gave rise to his sudden conviction that we were somehow the same.

"I want to hire your services, McNee."

"My services?"

"As an investigator. You want an 'in' so bad to my goddaughter's disappearance... well, here's your chance. An invite, as it were. I'll hold back nothing if she's recovered safely. You'll have whatever you need. Whatever fee you require." He turned back to face me, relaxed again, whatever fear he'd been hiding washed away as easily as the coffee down the drain.

"Working for you?"

"Is my money somehow worth less than anyone else's?"

I didn't know how to react. Settled for silence and stillness. Giving nothing away.

"You can think on it," he said. "I don't require an answer right away. But I know that you're not working for the reporter. That you're looking into this as a favour. He never paid you."

How did he know that?

"Whatever it costs, McNee."

I stood up. "Thanks for the coffee," I said. "I hope your goddaughter is found safe and well. But… respectfully… I decline to take on your case."

"May I ask why?"

"You can ask," I said. "But I'm not obliged to say."

Chapter 9

Driving away, I started slamming my fists against the steering wheel, roaring inside the confines of the car.

Torn between wanting to find the girl.

And wanting to find Burns guilty.

Of anything.

***

After the incident at the Western Necropolis where I had shot one man in self-defence, came close to killing another, it had been Susan who responded to the emergency call, who saved me from becoming a murderer.

I remember her riding with me in the back of the van. I was shivering from shock, my hand having been broken. She sat across from me, and when I think back on it I know that she wanted to reach out and offer comfort. But she was a professional. Had to let all of that go when she was on the job.

"Did it have to end like this?"

I didn't have a response to that.

"Why'd you even get involved in the first place?"

Did she really want me to answer?

She'd reached across, then, and touched my upper arm. I looked up, caught her eye, finally.

She said, "What is it about your life that means you take other people's business so personally? None of this needed to have involved you. You could have walked away from it all. So why didn't you?"

I didn't have an answer.

I guess I still don't.

***

From the office, I called Connolly.

"Tell me you have something."

"I'm backing out," I said.

I'd been thinking about it, driving back. Susan had said that I get involved in some cases because of guilt, not because they're a sound business decision or because the pay off is worth the risk.

She was right. If I wanted to live – and not just survive – I had to learn to distance myself from some things, to know when it was wise to step away.

I had to pay attention to my own life. Stop getting so deep in other people's affairs.

"We need to let the police handle this one," I said.

"They'll let you know when –"

"This could be an *exclusive*."

"No," I said, a little harsher than I meant to. "You're not my client. This was a favour, right? So this isn't my case. And I... I need to make a business decision. It's what I'm doing here. I'm walking away."

I slammed down the receiver before he had a chance to reply, walked over to the window and looked outside. Night had come fast, ink falling over the city. Orange street lights seemed to take on a strange haze, and I realised there was a gentle mist rolling in the streets.

I expected the phone to ring.

Connolly to call back with the offer of my standard fee plus expenses.

Never happened.

I decided to call it a night. Head home. Call Susan in the morning, tell her she didn't need to worry about me stepping on anyone's toes. I was listening to her for the first time in my life.

I was walking away.

It felt good.

At least, that's what I tried to convince myself of as I trudged out into the stairwell, ignoring the rising tightness in my chest and stomach and the nausea in my throat.

Walking down the stairs, my leg began to stiffen.

Old injury. One the doctors seemed unable to find a reason for. What was the word one of them had used? *Psychosomatic*?

Aye, what did they know?

"Steed."

I hadn't seen her, and she waited till my back was turned and I was locking up before she called my name.

I clicked the key home, turned and said, "I was thinking about you."

"Sounds romantic."

I shook my head.

"I should be so lucky," she said, with the kind of smile that I couldn't quite read.

"I'm walking away from this one," I said.

"The Furst case?"

"Aye."

"You never went to see Richie Harisson."

We walked down the stairs together. Slowly. Neither of us wanting to reach the bottom.

"Thing is… you have to look at why you take on a case. This one… there are elements that strike close to home. That threaten my… impartiality."

"You almost sound professional."

I grinned. Couldn't help it. "Almost."

At the foot of the stairs, before we hit the main door, she stopped, turned and leaned in. Kissed me briefly on the cheek, and when she pulled away I could still feel the ghost of her touch on my skin.

"You're doing the right thing, Steed," she said. "Maybe there's hope for you yet."

She slipped out the door and was gone before I could say anything.

I couldn't help but wonder why she'd come to see me. But maybe I'd saved her a speech.

I'd like to think so.

***

That night, I didn't sleep well.

No dreams. But I kept waking up. Anxious, like there was something I'd forgotten. I'd sit bolt upright, hit the bedside lamp and check the clock.

I'd wander around the flat for a while, maybe grab a drink before diving back under the covers, trying to get comfortable. And failing. Miserably.

Sleep took me at some point, but when I woke up again, it was as though I'd had no rest at all. My only clue that any time had passed was the light streaming between the curtains; brighter than it had been when I closed my eyes.

The clock provided another clue.

Half seven.

Sodit.

I showered and shaved. Stretched in the living room, listening to the radio.

Looking out the window, I could see a thin layer of snow covering the city. By mid-morning, it would be slush or maybe even gone, but somehow it seemed to have quieted the usual noises from outside. Traffic drove slower, the early morning voices were muted. The world was holding its breath.

I ate breakfast in front of the TV and took in next to nothing on the news.

Just past eight o'clock, the phone rang.

A rough voice on other end of the line, said, "McNee, you're going to want to come down to your wee office. Someone broke in last night. Gave the place a good going over. Real fucking mess, pal. Unless you need to employ better cleaning staff."

Christ, one of the last voices I needed to hear.

Chapter 10

DI George Lindsay was loitering on the pavement as I pulled into the nearest parking space. As little as a year ago, there was a car park across from the office, but they shut it down, built new university accommodation that looks like it'll collapse within the next five years.

Dundee's become one of those cities; filled with new money and dreaming of expansion. But as with all grand ideas, not all of them have been thought through. Some are plain eyesores and others are expensive mistakes; buildings that will barely stand five years never mind five hundred.

Hasn't the city learned from its mistakes? In the sixties and seventies, the council had knocked down grand old buildings to make way for imposing concrete designs that soon became ugly and outdated. Now they were knocking those down to make way for new buildings destined to become eyesores to the next generation.

No 1, Courthouse Square, wasn't so bad. Sandstone and refurbished in the late nineties, it was solid and interesting from the outside and beginning to age well enough. The bottom floors were occupied by a building society, and the entrance to the main stairwell which led to my own offices was round the side of the building.

I walked over to Lindsay, every step slow and deliberate. He grinned when he saw me, plucked the cigarette from between his lips and ground it out on the pavement.

"In case you're still living clean," he said. "Can't have an inconsiderate bastard like me offending the delicate sensibilities of an ex-smoker, aye?" First time we met was in the smoking room at Dundee FHQ over five years earlier, when you could still smoke indoors. I'd given up shortly after I met Elaine. Didn't miss it all that much.

Except when the habit itched.

Five years. The bastard had barely changed. Probably look the same at seventy as he did at fifty. He was short, with wide shoulders and the stance of a brawler. A large forehead, flat nose and tiny eyes that sparkled with a general hatred for everyone around him. He wore his suit reluctantly. Last thing you could accuse him of being was a clotheshorse

"How'd you catch the case?"

"Heard the call, couldn't resist."

Couldn't resist. Aye, couldn't resist coming down here to piss me about. Long ago I realised he actually enjoyed our mutual antagonism, treated it like a game. Even when I broke his nose – and you could still see the crooked bump right there at the bridge – he'd taken to the role of wronged victim with what seemed a childlike glee.

"They're keeping you away from the big boy cases," I said. "Figured you'd have been all over the

Mary Furst investigation."

He craned his neck to look up the third floor windows of my office. "You know, pal, it's a fucking mess up there."

"Tell me."

He turned his attention back to me. "They did a number, all right. Maybe you can help us figure what's missing. Whether they stole anything of value." He laughed at that; his own private joke.

I moved past him. He followed at a discreet distance. I didn't turn around, but still knew he was smirking.

The prick.

***

"Maybe you'd be better investing in security," he said as we came to the top of the stairs. "I mean, this isn't exactly good publicity for your services, aye? And we've done this dance before." Last time he came to my offices, he'd found a man bleeding out on the floor. The worst kind of timing.

I shot Lindsay the finger over my shoulder.

He hadn't been exaggerating about the mess. The door had been smashed off its hinges, the frame cracked and splintered. Inside, someone had emptied out every file, overturned the desk in reception.

I felt sick.

Remembered holding Bill as he bled out on the floor. Gut shot.

We'd been friends as much as colleagues. These days, after the incident, we barely spoke. The poor bastard was still in a wheelchair. His boyfriend blamed me for what had happened. I did as well.

65

Best not to think about it, of course. There was a long list of the dead and injured behind me. If I started taking personal responsibility for them all, there'd be no end to my litany of sins.

Lindsay whispered in my ear, "You're looking peaky." A cartoon devil whispering bad thoughts. I was missing the angel, of course.

Slipping away from him, I checked my private office. Again, the door smashed in, the tables overturned, the files emptied. The safe was on its side, the door blown open.

A message?

Maybe.

I knelt down beside the safe. Checked the outside. Saw the warped metal, the scorch marks.

"They knew what they were doing," said Lindsay. "This wasn't a bunch of wee neds breaking into someone's office for kicks, right?"

I closed my eyes. Pictured the explosion. Muffled, powerful. The door blowing off.

They knew what they were doing.

Who had those kinds of connections?

I said, "They were looking for something specific."

"In the safe?"

"I don't know. Maybe they were just trying every nook and cranny."

I felt my stomach cramp. Started flexing my fingers. Not quite making fists, but like I was wrapping them round some bastard's throat.

Aye, fuckit, I knew who had those kinds of connections.

Who'd think I had something up here worth nabbing.

Someone who'd already made their interest in my work known.

"You have a knack of pissing off the wrong people," Lindsay said. "How's the wee lad doing, anyway? The one who got shot?"

I got to my feet. Spun on heels to face Lindsay. My nails dug into the palms of my hands. My body was humming.

He saw it, and just for a moment he lost control. His eyes widened and he leaned away from me.

Aye, he pretended like he was in control, had nothing to fear. But the cocky wee shite was shaking in his boots.

Made me feel better.

Not much. But enough that I could walk away.

***

Another time, I might have been proud, just walking out of there. Not trying to throttle Lindsay.

Call me a changed man.

Or maybe the fight had been shocked out of me.

Whatever the case, I was down the stairs and out on the street again, one man on my mind.

Aye, maybe I walked out of there because I had some other arsehole to throttle.

Had to be Burns. No other shite would give a toss about my files. He'd offered me a job, and I'd refused it. All the same, I'd been working on a case that interested him. He wanted whatever I knew.

Did he think I was holding out on him?

That I knew something about his goddaughter I wasn't willing to share?

As I made to cross the road, a voice called, "McNee." Deep, heavy, enough to stop me cold.

I turned, saw a man I didn't recognise. Big guy. Dressed in a suit that seemed to pinch, as though there wasn't quite enough material to make him clothes that actually fit. But he wasn't fat. Even from a distance you could see the muscle. He sported the kind of beard that would make a lumberjack proud, and slicked his dark hair back from his temples. His eyes were wide, manic, made me think of Tom Baker who used to play the lead in *Doctor Who*.

I hesitated.

The big guy took it as his cue, came across. "You are McNee, then?"

"And you?"

He offered his hand. Bigger than a boxing glove. Christ, find yourself on the wrong end of that, you'd be in real trouble.

"Wickes," he said. Surprisingly, he didn't try and crush my hand. I'd been expecting it, bracing for it. Figured him for the kind of guy who'd like to show off his strength. But he had a strangely delicate shake. "I'm in the investigation game like yourself."

I nodded. Tried to think. I knew most of the local crowd by sight, even the ones who worked for larger firms. But the name Wickes had never come across my radar.

He said, "I work out of Glasgow mostly, but… d'you think we can talk?"

"I don't have the time."

"It's about the girl. The one who's missing."

Hard not to react to that one.

He said, "I think I know what happened to her."

***

We grabbed a table at the Washington Café on Union Street. The café had undergone a recent facelift, getting rid of the old booths and vinyl pews and replacing them with rounded tables and high backed chairs. I still wasn't sure what I thought about it, but the coffee was decent and we could talk in relative peace.

The radio on the counter spat out local stations; a mix of nostalgic pop music and local news.

Wickes got in the coffees, grabbed himself a bacon roll. I wasn't hungry, my stomach still churning from bad memories.

"I heard your name through the grapevine," he said as he slid in across the table from me. "Bad business you were involved in last year."

"Wrong place, wrong time."

Wickes laughed. An unnatural sound. Almost guttural. "I've heard that before."

I didn't bother defending myself or correcting him. Got the feeling he'd only hear what he wanted to.

Grand quality for an investigator.

"You said you knew something about Mary Furst."

"You're the man to talk to, right? Hear you're deeply involved with the investigation."

"I took an offer to look at the situation," I said. "But I'm not involved any longer. I backed off."

He sat back in his chair, deceptively casual. "You backed off? From a prize investigation like this? What, that business from before make you gunshy?"

I said nothing.

"Don't mean anything by it," he said after a moment. "I know your reputation. Your history. You're something of a celebrity. Unusual for an investigator." Christ, I didn't think I could cope with any kind of hero worship. Or inane flattery designed to get me on side.

"If you have information," I said, "you should go to the police. I know the investigating officers and –"

"Let me show you what I have," he said. "See if it changes your mind."

I sighed. This guy wasn't going to take no for an answer.

I figured at least he'd distracted me, stopped me doing something stupid. I owed him for that at least. And what harm could it do to hear him out?

Even then, I was still fooling myself. Thinking over and over: *I am no longer involved with this case. I'm taking the high road. Taking responsibility for my actions*

Aye. Right.

Chapter 11

Sixteen years ago, a woman – at that time, more a girl – named Deborah Brown agreed to surrogate for a couple struggling to conceive.

Not the kind of decision anyone makes lightly. You don't rush it, go in half-arsed. No. You go slow. Make the right decisions. Ensure that everyone knows where they stand.

Contracts have to be drawn up. Surrogacy is not illegal in the UK, but there are measures in place to ensure that everyone is happy. That no one gets hurt.

Beyond the obvious, of course.

It's a simple business on paper. What you're doing is renting a womb. In theory, it's letting out a flat for nine months or giving someone a loan of your car.

Except it's not.

Because when it comes to people's bodies, emotions follow fast.

I don't know that I ever really wanted children. I certainly used to argue with Elaine about it.

Susan once asked me why, when we'd been

together so long, me and Elaine never even considered starting a family.

I didn't tell Susan about the fights we had.

Or why Elaine had become distracted in the moments before our car was knocked off the road and she was killed.

That conversation about…

Children.

Like I said, people get emotional.

Watching Wickes tell me about this woman, Deborah Brown, I noted how he lit up. Something dancing in his eyes when he mentioned her name.

Investigations require dispassionate distance. He'd lost his with this woman.

Deborah Brown.

Mary Furst's birth mother.

Aye, that's the part that knocked me flat on my arse as well.

***

The problem lay with Jennifer Furst. She'd suffered traumatic surgery in her youth: having a child could kill her. No joke, no slim chance.

A real heartbreaker for someone who thought about nothing except family. In her youth, Jennifer had believed that a family of her own would end all her problems. She would become a real human being, a fully rounded person.

Talk about buying into the myth.

Surrogacy seemed a sensible option. But she realised the risks of asking a close friend or anyone they knew to act as the surrogate. So she and her husband set out to find someone.

A difficult task.

Like I said, while surrogacy isn't illegal in the UK, there are measures in place.

You can't advertise. Either that you're looking for a surrogate or that you wish to be one.

Maybe I can understand the reasons for that. Any industry based on such a personal matter would be open to all kinds of disastrous loopholes.

All the same, they searched for someone.

That someone turned out to be Deborah Brown.

Deborah was eighteen years old at the time. An art student facing expulsion and bankruptcy. Looking for a way out. Something that could help her get back on track.

Jennifer spent time with Deborah. The two of them became close. Built a relationship of trust.

One of the things you learn fast in my line of business is that trust is an overhyped virtue. Relationships can fall apart with the smallest of cracks.

Later, Deborah would say that she thought they had become closer than sisters.

She'd be wrong, of course.

***

"There's something you're holding back."

He shook his head. "But you see where this is going?"

"Deborah was important to you. You were close to her."

He nodded. Closed his eyes, and kept his hands on top of the table. Rocked gently in his chair, keeping time to some melody only he could hear. "Close to her? I loved her."

73

***

The pregnancy itself was uneventful.

The two women – Jennifer and Deborah – spent a lot of time together. Maybe more than they should have. Part of the agreement drawn up stated that after the baby was born, Deborah would sever all ties with the family.

Closer than sisters?

Chalk that up to delusional.

I could see Jennifer Furst's point of view. For her, it was a business arrangement. She got what she wanted. Deborah got what she wanted. Everyone was happy.

"Deborah was looking for a family," I said.

Wickes nodded. "She wasn't close to her parents, then. Had a sister, but even if the lass kept an eye out for Deborah, they weren't close. The sister never had Deborah's best interests at heart." He closed his eyes again. Close to tears? Hard to imagine this giant of a man welling up, but I could feel it in the same way you sometimes feel a storm coming over the hill.

Hearing Wickes tell me the story, I reckoned that things had got complicated before the ink on that agreement was even dry.

Any agreements between surrogates and parents are private. They cannot be upheld in a court of law.

In Scotland we have a law of verbal contract. All it takes is for two people to state their intent and the agreement is binding. There are grey areas, of course. This was one of them.

As the birth grew closer, Jennifer started to back off from her friendship. Treating the whole thing professionally; a transaction and little more.

Deborah didn't take too kindly to the cooling off of what she thought was a close friendship. Put this down to her being younger than Jennifer?

Maybe.

Or maybe she was just more innocent.

That's the way Wickes played it up in his version of events. Like Deborah wasn't cynical enough to grasp what was really going on.

I've been around long enough to realise that there is no such thing as pure innocence. That naivety is more often a cover than a truth.

Made me wonder why Wickes was making such a conscious effort to fool me. And himself.

I loved her.

Aye, love'll do funny things to a person, right enough.

When Mary was born, everything happened according to the agreement. The parental order was signed, meaning that Deborah Brown was no longer Mary's legal mother, even if her name would still appear on the birth certificate.

Jennifer Furst expected Deborah would just back off.

Take the money and run.

Like I said, these things have a habit of getting complicated.

Chapter 12

"When she saw Mary for the first time, it was… a religious experience. Her words." Wickes was holding his coffee in both hands. Had raised it a few times close to his lips, but he hadn't actually drunk anything. By now it would be cold.

He hadn't been thirsty. Just needed a prop.

I sat back and listened.

A good investigator doesn't talk. He prompts. Listens to what people have to say, knowing they naturally want to open up. They'll do it without thinking if you give them the opportunity. No matter how much they'll consciously deny the impulse.

I wonder if the Catholics have the right idea: confession is good for the soul. Everybody needs someone to talk to.

Wickes's eyes were damp; filming over. Was the big man coming close to tears? Seemed unlikely, but you're a fool if you think you know anyone within five minutes of meeting them. He was talking about Deborah after the birth, "Holding this wee life in her hands. Realising that it came from within her…"

Talking like they were his own feelings. Like he knew this woman so completely, there was no need to separate her emotions from his.

It worried me a little.

Then again, I'd been called a heartless bastard before. Maybe I just couldn't understand the depth of his empathy.

If I didn't jump in, help him a little, I feared he might break down. I wasn't ready to cope with that.

"So suddenly the business arrangement didn't seem so important."

He smiled, nodded. "You get it, then?"

"Guess so."

Except I didn't. Not really.

Wickes had this strange look about him. A smile that was blurred by an odd regret.

Love makes you believe foolish things.

Impossible things.

Thinking you'll know that one person forever is just the beginning of your delusions.

My job was to separate Wickes's raw emotions from the facts. Distil what he told me until I could properly understand the situation.

I had the feeling he already knew the truth,

Needed someone else to bring it out for him.

***

Deborah didn't want to give up the rights to her child.

She tried to push the matter, pleaded with Jennifer Furst. Asked for some access – any access – to Mary's life. When she told Wickes about it, she said, "You won't ever understand it. But you carry this life inside you for nine months, you form a connection. A bond that no one else can understand. Separation is the hardest part. You don't want to let go. You can't."

Jennifer Furst didn't understand, believing that getting Deborah more deeply involved with Mary's life was asking for disaster.

I didn't have all the details. Just a rambling third hand account from a second hand source who was too emotionally involved to give me the dispassionate facts I needed.

But I could fill in the blanks.

What was obvious was that the Fursts had rushed into things. OK, they made sure they'd crossed the i's and dotted the t's on the paperwork, but what they hadn't done was properly screen their choice for surrogate.

As in, psychological evaluation.

Emotionally speaking, would Deborah Brown be able to handle carrying a child to term and then giving it up?

Wickes may have been in love with Deborah – so he kept telling me – but even he was willing to admit that she had problems.

"She was a depressive as a teenager. The kind of kid who contemplated suicide."

"Self harm?"

"Nothing that left a lasting impression."

"But something?"

He didn't seem willing to answer. As though he'd be admitting to something he didn't want to hear himself.

I pushed: *"But something?"*

Aye, something.

A laundry list. Depression. Eating disorders. Mood swings.

The kind of problems that don't just go away.

78

I got the sense there was a great deal Wickes wasn't telling me.

My gut said it was because he wanted to protect Deborah. Didn't want to dirty her name any more than he had to.

"Why did you come to me?"

He straightened, scraped his chair back a few inches away from the table.

"What?"

"You approached me," I said. "You knew who I was. Came to my office. To talk about this. Said you knew about what had happened to Mary. Why? Why not go to the police?"

"I didn't want them involved –"

"You're being naïve," I said. He had to hear the truth from someone. Who better than a dispassionate observer.

"Aye?"

"Or you're leaving something out." I was pushing him. Had to.

He took a deep breath, turned away.

I said, "You want to tell me. We wouldn't be here if you didn't."

He nodded, turned back to look at me. Held it. "Doesn't sound so bad, aye? A mother wanting to be reunited with her daughter."

I nodded. "But the girl's gone."

"The girl's gone."

Something in his face. His lips twitched. "We had this dog," he said. "We had this fucking dog, and she loved it. Spoiled the little bastard completely. And… the poor creature… got into the fridge. Because of a fucking chicken. A bone got caught up in the digestive system. I don't know… I mean, something to do with its kidneys… whatever, the wee thing was going to die. Painfully, you know?"

"Had to be put down?"

"Aye. I made an appointment with the vets, came back to get the poor bastard. But it was gone. She... she wouldn't tell me where it was. Said it had run away, must have known what was going to happen to it."

I said, "It didn't run away," filling in the gaps.

He shook his head. "I woke up, found she wasn't in bed." He hesitated, seemed to think of something. Clarified by adding: "By then, we were close." He was hesitant, searching for the right words. I got the meaning. "She wasn't there, and... I went to look for her."

I was the one who broke eye contact this time.

"Found her in the cupboard in the hall. Sitting in the dark. With the dog's corpse. She'd poisoned it. Rather than let someone else do the deed."

"She poisoned her own dog?"

"Hid it in the cupboard. So that no one would find it. She was so attached to the fucking animal that she would rather kill it and keep it to herself than let anyone help."

I nodded.

Understood what he was telling me.

She loved the dog. Couldn't part with it.

Maybe love wasn't the right word. I got the feeling Wickes was steering me towards, *obsessed*.

She didn't let go easily?

Try *at all*.

Chapter 13

"Tell me where you came in to the picture."

He hesitated. Started looking around. The café was beginning to fill up. Maybe he was worried that someone was watching.

Like who?

He seemed satisfied, dropped his head again and said, "Maybe six months after the lass was born." He looked ready to start glancing about again. Then gave me an explanation for his sudden attack of nerves. "You know about Jennifer Furst's family, of course?"

"Oh, aye. I've had my dealings with... Mary's god-father."

Always came back to that bastard. I tried not to let Wickes see how I felt about Burns.

Wickes said, "He's something of a legend, aye?"

I shrugged. "They say a lot of things about David Burns. If only half of them are true –"

"– Then he's the devil himself." Wickes looked around the café, as though coming out of sleep, realising where he was. Caught the eye of the wee waitress, waved her over and ordered a fresh coffee. She looked at his mug with a strange expression as though she couldn't figure why he hadn't finished the last one.

When she went away, Wickes turned his attention back to me. My own coffee had been finished minutes earlier, and I still had my hands wrapped around the mug. Must have looked as though I was afraid to let go. My fingers were whitening with the pressure.

Wickes started talking again. "In fairness to her, Jennifer Furst didn't have much to do with that side of the family. Least, it's the way things used to be. She thought of herself as a decent citizen. Law abiding."

Everyone does.

Until they cross the line.

And one thing being a copper taught me: at some point, everyone crosses the line.

***

Would it sound like tit-for-tat to say that Deborah was first? Her behaviour shifting from insistence to harassment.

Even Wickes couldn't sugar coat it, and emotionally involved as he was he still had the detachment to tell me outright everything that Deborah had done.

Phone calls. Standing outside the house. Following Jennifer and the child to the shops.

And finally, breaking and entering. Coming through a window at night and sneaking upstairs to the baby's room.

The husband found her in there, standing over

Mary's crib and making soft, cooing noises. "To help the baby sleep."

Sometimes it's not what other people do to us that hurts the most, but what we do to ourselves.

I could understand Deborah. How she felt. Had some sense of her reluctance to let go. But she had known what she was getting into. Must have done. Wickes had gone into detail, told me everything about the surrogate arrangement. How it was all above board. Utterly transparent.

I couldn't help thinking about the dog. About Deborah sitting in the dark, holding its corpse, unable to let go.

Charges should have been pressed against Deborah. The way Wickes told it, Jennifer refused to proceed with pressing criminal charges and the situation was settled, "with a few words."

And still... Deborah persisted. Continued to try and insinuate herself into the child's life.

"When she came to me, she was a mess," Wickes said. "Told me all of this. Nearly broke down, you see. Jesus fuck." He wiped at his face as though batting away tears. Maybe the ones I'd seen earlier making another attempt to break through. "I mean, she was a state."

What did she tell him?

She told him all that he had told me.

Told him that after the courts slapped her on the wrist, she kept trying. Believing she was a woman getting fucked by the system.

Mary was *her* child, and she knew it now, she'd make a better mother than the girl's legal guardians.

Surrogacy be fucked.

Mary needed her mother. Deborah knew this – *felt*

it – from the inside out.

Deborah snatched the baby. In broad daylight.

"She had no control," said Wickes. "Over her own actions."

Jennifer didn't call the police.

No, she went to her husband's uncle.

David Burns.

"All things considered," Wickes said, "The bastard was gentle as a lamb."

Gentle as a lamb. Aye, sure, if that lamb shared traits with Hannibal Lecter.

Even fifteen years ago, Burns had the kind of reputation that meant he no longer had to lift a finger. He gave the nod, a whole squad of would-be hardmen jumped to attention.

The daylight snatch was resolved fast. Deborah had moved back in with her sister. Had taken the baby there. Christ, I could only imagine her reaction when the hard men came round to "persuade" her to give back the kid.

I had to ask: "Did the sister know?"

"Must have," he said. Skipping over the subject like he wasn't sure.

Or he didn't want to tell me.

I wasn't there when the men came for the child. Neither was Wickes.

But he talked like he was. As though he'd been there. Watched the whole damn sorry affair unfold. And maybe he'd heard the story enough he could come to believe that he had been.

***

Deborah had let herself in earlier that day using the spare key her sister had given her. She was sleeping in an upstairs box room on a fold out bed. She didn't have many possessions. Had a few boxes that she left unpacked. Because she didn't want her sister to see what she had in there.

Baby clothes. Toys. All the shite she'd have bought for her own baby.

No, she still couldn't accept that Mary wasn't "her" child. That it wasn't as simple as who gave birth to the girl. That she had no claim, not after the paperwork had gone through declaring the Fursts as Mary's legal guardians.

She took the baby upstairs, wrapped in the blanket she had grabbed when she took Mary out of the stroller.

Feeling ashamed of herself, even then. Or at least that's what she would later tell Wickes, that she knew what she was doing was wrong.

Yet did it anyway.

Did that make her a bad person? Or just sick in some way?

These were the questions she asked herself. Maybe that hinted at an answer. I couldn't really say for sure.

She laid the baby on the fold out bed. On top of the thick blankets her sister had pulled out of a cupboard a few days ago.

Mary Furst, barely six months old, gurgled happily. She didn't cry. Hadn't done since Deborah had snatched her. The baby understanding that this was her mother. That this woman didn't mean her any harm.

"And she didn't. You understand?" Wickes snapped the question into his narrative with an intensity that could have knocked me off my seat.

Did he expect me to judge?

Or was he trying to convince himself?

Whatever the case, Deborah was upstairs with the baby. Digging into boxes. Looking for something she could give the baby. Something that would make it appear as though Mary was truly her daughter, now. Nothing was ever going to separate them.

The baby gurgled. The baby squirmed.

Deborah wanted to cry. Couldn't say for sure whether this feeling was good or bad. Just that it overwhelmed her; made her want to break down and cry.

That was around the same time she heard the noise from downstairs. The door breaking in. Wood splintering.

Male voices shouting. Their words indistinct.

Footsteps on the stairs.

***

Wickes couldn't continue.

As though there was something he didn't want to say.

I guessed at it. Maybe just knew instinctively.

I pressed the issue. Said, "She tried to kill the baby." Bad interview technique. You never push the subject in a direction. You never put words in their mouths. But I was acting like we were on a deadline here. Like this was my case. But I'd given it up. Right?

Wickes said, "She's not a bad person."

I nodded. "If she couldn't have it…"

He finished for me' "…then no one could." I was giving him the cues here. Against every professional instinct. "She was ill," he said. "You know that, right? The kind of ill you don't get better from." He tapped the side of his head. Not with a sense of distaste or mockery, but reinforcing the point. "Up here. They don't have medicines that work, you know. Not really. The last few years, we tried a lot of things. I wanted her to get better. To be well again. You have to know that. You have to understand."

For a moment, I didn't know for sure whether he was still talking about Deborah Brown.

Couldn't bring myself to ask.

***

I'd dealt with Burns's thugs before. Subtlety wasn't their strong suite. He picked his lads for loyalty and ferociousness, not for their conversation or their Mensa applications.

Their brief had been simple:

Get the baby. Persuade Deborah that she wasn't wanted round these parts.

Be thankful for small mercies; they left Deborah alive. Battered and bruised, aye. But still breathing. They took the child – crying, Wickes said, as they separated her from her mother – and left.

On their way out the door, one of them said to her, "The boss sends us back here again and we'll fucking kill you."

His friend added, with eloquence: "Cunt."

Wickes hesitated as he told me this story. Stumbled over the words. They upset him, somehow. Perhaps because of Deborah; he didn't want to think about what had happened to her.

All things considered, Deborah's injuries were relatively minor. Her sister came back home to find Deborah sitting on the end of her fold out bed, legs tucked up to her chest, face bloodied, eyes blackened.

She was left with a sprained wrist, a broken rib and enough lumps that they couldn't lie to the hospital, couldn't say she'd had some kind of accident.

"It became a mugging. The sister – and this was the only time she ever really came through for Deborah – she understood what would happen if either of them went to the police."

Deborah stopped leaving the house. Became paranoid. Sank further into her own depression.

"And you asked," Wickes said. "So I'm telling you. That's where I came in."

Chapter 14

"I had ideals," Wickes said. "Don't get me wrong." He was talking about his own career. Putting me in the picture.

Confession is good for the soul, right?

I was curious what he had to confess.

Ideals.

I got into this gig so I could lose myself in other people's lives. But maybe I was deluding myself when I talked about making the world a better place, providing some kind of truth.

Ideals.

They're what people expect you to have. What you use to excuse your real motivations.

Wickes's ideals were sound, maybe even a tad more romantic than I'd expect from the burly man who sat across the other side of the table. He got into the investigation business to help people.

I couldn't sense guile or deceit, and he met my gaze straight on. Did I believe him? It was hard not to.

"Truly," he said, and gestured, "Hand on heart."

He straightened his back, closed his eyes, held the pose melodramatically for a moment before relaxing. "Sounds like a bad joke, right enough. But we were all young and principled once. Right?"

That last word made me flinch, maybe even look away. Did he catch that? See past my composure for a moment? I would have, I knew it.

What Wickes found, the deeper he got into the business, was that he had a talent for finding people. He started working with another investigator in Glasgow, learned in a kind of unofficial apprenticeship. "A lot of security work. I've never been the wee man, you can probably tell. Guess I looked like a goon, whatever. He had me work the rackets. The kind of jobs I guess someone like you wouldn't even consider." He smiled at me. Vaguely condescending. Did he mean it to be? I wasn't sure.

"These days, you lads are minted and trained and shaped and moulded. Told right and wrong, what you can and cannot do. Back in my day… we had no national organisation. We weren't monitored by bastards like the Security Industry Authority. No, we learned the trade on the streets. Christ, why would you even think about organising a business like ours? Once it becomes respectable, the services people require are impossible to provide."

There was a strange air of nostalgia to his voice. A pining for days long lost. Not for the innocence, but for a power and influence that had eluded Wickes in later years.

His early work was in enforcement. His word, not mine. He didn't seem to shy away from it or try and disguise the work as anything other than it was. He dissuaded abusive husbands, confronted philanderers, made straight up calls for debts that needed collection. As time went on, he started to demon-strate an aptitude for tracing the disappeared.

"I went into business for myself somewhere around 1997," he said. "*Wickes Investigations*. Above board. Got myself registered with the local police. Didn't join the Association, but that was laziness more than anything, you know? I specialised in trace and debt collection." He smiled. "And other jobs, off the record."

Deborah came to him through a recommendation. He didn't give me the specifics, and honestly, I didn't ask. His past was his past.

Did it matter? Not for what I wanted to know.

We all have our sins. Our mistakes. Not all of them reach out to the present.

Chapter 15

"When she came to see me, I got that spark. You know the spark?" Wickes paused, fixed those wild eyes on me, looking for something. Nodded, more to himself than me. "Aye, you know the spark," he said, "Can see that, at least. Wife?"

I held up my hand. No ring. Said, "She died."

Wickes nodded, looking serious again. "Well, this lass, I guess you felt the spark with her. Electric. First time I saw her, I thought I was going to have a heart attack."

I didn't want to disillusion him.

First time I saw Elaine, I was thinking, *here's another drunk driver* and then was glad to see someone sober roll down the window.

No sparks.

Maybe a connection, though. Tender. Fragile. Fleeting. One that would build, evolve, become something else entirely.

I'm not sure I believe in love at first sight. I think sometimes we want to see it; we fall in love with being in love. Retrospectively we create that fantasy of instant chemistry, desire, attraction. But the truth is, that kind of immediate spark with another person, that absolute certainty that here is the person for you... no, I can't believe in it. Love builds. Grows. Evolves.

I didn't say any of this to Wickes.

People don't like having their beliefs challenged.

"So I helped her. Because I couldn't say no. Not to this woman. Not with her story."

He admitted fully that this was done, at least in part, for selfish reasons. "Did I know it at the time? Fuck knows, eh? We don't always have the idea why we do anything. No one knows nothing, eh? I just had this feeling that I needed her near me. That we were supposed to be together. You know what I'm talking about, don't you? Not that I want to bring up bad feelings, but you remember?"

"I remember." And maybe I did at that.

He told me how he kept her close. Protected her. The cynical part of me thought it sounded as though he had made her dependant upon him.

It was what she asked for, after all. She came to him for protection. Looking for a way out.

How could he refuse?

But I dismissed the idea that he somehow twisted their relationship; manipulated her into falling for him the same way he had for her. Sure, he was over the top and maybe a little too in touch with his emotions, but there was something about him I liked. He appeared innocent in his beliefs, and the twinkle in his eye when he laughed... maybe that's what Deborah had finally fallen in love with.

He talked like it was an instant thing, their love affair, but I sensed it took time and maybe even a little coercion on his part. And sometimes I got the impression that even he realised how ludicrous he sounded. Just a dip of the head here or a shift of the gaze there that told me he was self-editing.

Touching as it was, his story was drifting. Two cups of coffee, both gone cold. If we had all the time in the world, I might have let him keep talking. But at the centre of this story, there was a missing girl. She couldn't afford to wait.

I said, "Tell me how all of this connects to Mary Furst. Her disappearance."

And that's when he hesitated.

Never a good sign.

***

It started out with little things. Temper tantrums that were wildly out of proportion with what started them. Melodramatic behaviour. He'd come home late, she'd throw a plate at his head. The phone would ring, she'd start to tear up as though she thought death was on the other end of the line.

Wickes let it pass for the first few months. Who could blame her for being paranoid? After what Burns's hired muscle had put her through she had every right to nerves and anxiety. These would disappear in time. Wickes was sure of that.

Except they didn't.

They got worse.

"She became a different person. Started to live out this paranoid fantasy life. Self harming." He blinked a few times in rapid succession. I couldn't see a trace of tears or broken capillaries in his whites. "Telling me someone else did it even when I knew that there was nobody who could have. She would leave the house without telling me where she was going." He talked like she'd escaped, broken the walls of some compound.

How close was the protection he offered?

Even he had to admit that perhaps it was too close. Smothering, maybe. "You ever had that moment of clarity? When you realise that you were in the wrong all the time?" He told me with no hint of self-deprecation or regret about what he did to make her feel better.

"That's when I bought her the dog."

That was when it became clear to Wickes that any attempt to substitute for the child she had lost was doomed to failure. Maybe even made her behaviour worse.

He started to spend more time at home. Became worried for her state of mind, started to fear that she might somehow kill herself.

It was art that finally saved her. "That's what she did before, when she was at university, before all of this crap took over her life. She was an art student. Duncan of Jordanstone, the art college. She was good, too. Know when they call someone promising? Aye, she was that and more."

Wickes took the credit for reawakening her interest. "It saved her. Externalised all the shite she bottled up inside, you know? Her fear. Her need to make up for what she saw as her mistakes." He stopped talking, cocked his head to one side as though thinking back on what he just said. "I sound like a psychologist, right?"

Without thinking, I corrected him: "A psychiatrist."

That seemed to unnerve him. Struck some chord. Maybe he hadn't expected me to know what he was talking about.

He hid a lot behind the jokes and bluster.

Maybe more than I'd realised.

But the slip lasted only a moment. And then he was talking like nothing had happened. Just pushing through, maybe hoping I'd get caught in his slipstream, start to doubt I'd even observed the hesitation.

He told me how he persuaded her to start painting again. Encouraged her to apply to a local art college and finish her training. Get her teaching degree.

"She needed a life. She'd come to rely on me completely. I ask, is that healthy?" The hint of a laugh on the horizon, but it never came.

Deborah got a job. Art teacher at a Glasgow High School.

Her vocation.

Wickes told me how she appeared to finally put the memories of her daughter behind her. Their lives started to approach normal. "I loved her," he said. "I love her. All I wanted was for us to be together."

I expected him to add, "and for her to be happy," but he didn't.

Of course, nothing good ever lasts. About five years later, he realised that the lies had started again. Little things. Inconsistencies and hesitations in her stories. They seemed insignificant at first but took on more weight with their consistency.

She began working longer hours. Attending more after school conferences. Leaving earlier in the morning.

He did some work. Put that old training into practice. Aye, he wasn't affiliated, but it didn't mean he wasn't an investigator, didn't have the skills.

He found out that she'd transferred schools. From Glasgow to Dundee. Back to the city she told him she'd left behind.

No wonder she was working longer hours. Taking all these trips out of town. "I shouldn't have let her out of my sight," he said, and there was a tremor in his voice that should have been regret but came across as harder and more vicious. Subtle enough, I couldn't be sure if I'd imagined it.

"You know the work," he said. "It takes time. And I didn't want to be wrong. Didn't want to accuse her of anything, maybe kick off more problems. Who knew why she was coming back, right? So I tried to keep it on the QT. Figured maybe she got a transfer, didn't want to tell me because she knew what I might think. It's been fourteen years. I doubted that eejit Burns even remembered who she was, eh? And then… I got a look at her email account. Broke in, found out she'd been in touch with the girl. With Mary."

I nodded. Could figure where this was going.

"I was going to confront her before I realised she was gone. Last email on the account, she had arranged to meet the girl a few hours before she was reported as missing."

"She give a location?"

"Oh, aye." Wickes shook his head, a gesture of disappointment more than a contradiction. "The train station, you believe that? I was only twelve hours too late."

By the time he got there, she was long gone.

And, of course, so was Mary Furst.

Her daughter.

The baby she'd never really been able to let go off. To forget.

I couldn't help thinking of Deborah in the dark, cradling the corpse of the dog she had killed.

Hoping she could tell the difference between a pet and a human being.

Chapter 16

We finished our coffee, took a walk through the town centre. Stopped in the City Square, shadowed by the Caird Hall. Someone once told me how the square had been used as a double for St Petersberg when the British film industry was in full swing. Was it true? Sometimes it's hard to distinguish local rumour from actual history. But a brief glance at the austere architecture and you might believe it.

The weather had turned fair but brisk and people seemed in a hurry to get where they were going. Some walked cautiously along the cobbled pedestrian area outside the eastern doors of the Overgate shopping centre. The ice on the ground was invisible; one of nature's more frivolous little jokes.

Wickes walked to one of the fountains in the square, passed his large hands through a jet of water. Shivered. "Should have bloody known, eh? But maybe you can't help people like Deborah. I mean, not really help them," he said. "The people with scars that'll never heal."

I watched him as he passed his hands back and forth through the water. His eyes were in shadow, as though he was trying to hide something from me. He hunched his shoulders; defeated.

I still couldn't figure his sudden mood swings. Upbeat and laughing one moment, the weight of the world pressing down on him the next.

I figured: stress. Worry. Fear.

Things I could relate to.

He felt responsibility for what had happened to Mary Furst, even if he wasn't to blame.

Susan had made similar accusations to me before. Tearing her hair out as she tried to tell me how I couldn't solve the world's problems. How I wasn't the single catalyst for all the bad shit that happened in people's lives.

Things look different from the outside.

He said, "You know what I'm asking, don't you?"

"I've done what I can on this case," I said. "I don't have a client. Only reason I came anywhere near it was a favour to a friend."

He nodded. Hunched further, shoved his hands into his coat pockets. "You're going to make me ask?"

I didn't say anything.

"I don't know the city. I've not worked a case in years. And I know I'm too close to Deborah to get the kind of distance…"

"I told you –"

"The cost doesn't matter."

I sighed. "There are reasons I can't –"

"I don't think she wants to hurt the girl," Wickes said. "But I can't take responsibility for what she might –"

"Go to the police."

He swung round. "You know I can't. I want this to end quietly. I want it all to go away. I know I can't pretend it never happened, but I… maybe I can make it right."

I tried to turn away.

Thinking about the dead dog.

About the look in Wickes's eyes when he talked about Deborah.

What else did I have going on?

Why was I so reluctant?

Because I knew how badly this could end?

Because I'd promised Susan I'd play things straight these days, wouldn't throw myself into hopeless and suicidal cases?

Wickes reached inside his jacket, pulled out his wallet. Peeled notes from inside.

Two hundred quid in twenties.

He held them out. In broad daylight.

"Whatever else you need," he said. "I have to fix this. Can't help feeling like it's all somehow my fault."

I looked at the outstretched hand.

I nodded.

"But we play by my rules," I said. "It gets out of hand, we take what we know to the police." I licked my lips. "Okay?"

He smiled.

I took the cash. Said, "So we go to the office, do this right."

He stepped forward. For a moment, I thought he was going to hug me. The idea was terrifying. His build, he could crush me.

But he didn't. He just said, "We'll find her." And then he turned away from me, and the brisk wind stole something mumbled from his mouth. And if I didn't know better, I might have thought the words were, "We'll find the bitch."

Chapter 17

After Wickes signed the client contracts in the office, I told him I had other business to take care of. We agreed to meet in a couple of hours, swap notes, figure a way forward. Wickes said he had some of his own leads to follow up.

I climbed in the car on the street outside the office, idled for a few minutes, playing over my conversation with Wickes. Not the details of what he said but how he said it.

Telling myself I'd imagined that last mumbled phrase outside the Caird Hall, that the noise of the fountains had distorted his words, that my own paranoia was playing tricks on me.

I wanted to like the big man. Couldn't say why for sure, but something about his story clicked with me. The idea of a man trying to make right his own mistakes: something I could relate to.

But you can't always go on your gut.

After hearing more than my share of lies, I know that what you listen to in any confession or story is not the details of what someone says, but the way in which they tell you. You keep an ear out for trigger words, watch for signs of stress or anticipation, pay attention to patterns of words or tremors in tone and delivery.

It's not a science so much as an art. That old rumour about someone looking to the left when they're lying is so much horseshit, even if it is based on a kind of half-truth.

Wickes was lying to me about something. I think he believed almost everything he told me, but some part of him was either holding back or covering up. That was what unnerved me, made me start to question things I would otherwise have overlooked.

The casual rapport that he displayed felt deliberate, maybe even a little cynical. His entire demeanour was designed to play against his physical appearance; that hulking body, those huge hands, those staring eyes.

Aye, there was the rub.

Can we judge a man on the way he looks?

Like fuck.

If we did, then a man like Wickes would be a monster. And a man like David Burns would be a hardworking family man.

I drifted.

Thinking about Wickes's story.

Deborah Brown.

Mary Furst.

David Burns.

That bastard always coming back round. Always involved.

I roared and punched the steering wheel with my right hand. All pretence at calm and collected lost.

Wickes had his masks.

I had mine.

Why had I taken this case?

I don't know that even I could answer that for sure.

***

Ten months earlier.

My hand was aching. I made experimental moves, testing the boundaries of pain.

Curiosity as much as masochism.

Susan sat across the other side of the room, cradling her mug of tea in both hands and blowing at the surface to cool it down.

I wasn't looking at her. Not directly.

"You really mean that?" she asked.

I could have kicked myself. Opening up, even for a moment. What the hell else was she going to say?

I kept trying to flex my fingers individually. The tight wrap of the plaster made the movement difficult. The pain had centred on the palm.

If I closed my eyes, I could picture the moment all those broken bones, with a clarity that made me worry about what kind of dreams I'd face if I fell asleep.

The rain falling from the sky. Each individual drop visible. The shadow of a man standing over me, his foot stomping down hard.

My hand tried to spasm.

Couldn't quite manage it.

"Tell me, Steed."

I looked up at her, finally. Said, "I've thought about it."

"So tell me what good it'd do."

"I'd feel a lot fucking better for one thing."

She nodded. Had this half-smile.

Christ, of course it wouldn't.

It wasn't supposed to.

But what else do you do with anger? I'd been raging inside for over a year, searching in vain for someone who deserved this hate, who could be the signifier of everything that was wrong in the world.

All I wanted was revenge against someone whose crimes I couldn't even state.

David Burns was as good a man as any.

Which is why I'd told Susan the truth: one day, I was going to kill the bastard.

Even if I knew I'd never gain any satisfaction. Even if I already understood the futility of my anger.

"A month ago, you told me everything was different."

"He's a fucking criminal, Susan. The worst of his kind. He does whatever the fuck he wants and gets away with it."

"And he gets you to do his dirty work?"

I went silent.

Better than a slap.

What she said was true. Burns had set me up a couple of months earlier, seen my anger and recognised it for what it was. Set me on two London hard men in the hope that my anger would do the job he required. It had nearly worked, too.

And I had killed a man. Self defence or not, I couldn't escape that. A man who deserved to die. And still felt no satisfaction.

So what would happen if I killed Burns?

Would the anger inside fade away?

Or would it become hungrier and more insistent?

Susan stood up, came across and placed her hand

on top of mine. I couldn't feel her through the bandages.

"Move on, Steed," she said.

If only it was so easy.

***

I pulled up outside David Burns's house just past lunchtime. Noticed a car in the drive. Black BMW. Recently washed.

Aye, he may have been torn up inside with concern for his goddaughter, but like fuck was he going to appear slovenly.

I crunched the path to the front door, rang the bell.

The big man himself answered. "Can't stay away, can you?" He was dressed casual; open-necked blue shirt, white chinos and brown slip-on shoes. Made him appear genial, but his stance still had the hunch of the hard-man. Always on the alert, waiting for the next threat.

"Inside," I said. "We need to talk."

"I've got guests."

"To fuck with them."

He grinned, made me feel like I was a child throwing a tantrum. Nothing serious in what I said. All a big joke to Burns.

"We need to talk," I said again. "Can do it out here if you like." A challenge? Aye, and he knew it.

He turned and gestured. "Out back, then," he said. "Away from the twitching curtains of old busybodies across the street, eh?"

I turned to look, saw blinds move.

Street like this, of course they'd be watching his house. Better entertainment than a Saturday night on the telly.

***

Out back, Burns lit a cigar. "Call it my luxury," he said. "More so now the wife's gone on a healthy living kick." He grinned. "You don't strike me as a smoker. Else I'd offer one."

"I quit," I said.

He nodded, like I'd told a good, dry joke.

Blood thumped in my ears. Made me dizzy. "I told you yesterday that I don't want anything to do with you."

He smiled. Took a puff of the cigar. Casual. "And here you are… Your lips say no-no, but your eyes…" He let the joke hang.

I bulldozed past it."You know why I'm here."

His puzzled expression could have won an Academy award. "No. I don't, McNee. That's the honest truth." I had to wonder how much he was fighting the temptation to raise a hand to his heart in mock-seriousness. Just to rub it the fuck in.

"The break in… you're telling me it had nothing to do with you?"

"I'm a business man. I don't know why –"

"Don't give me that shite," I said. "Don't fucking start, okay? Just… *fuck!*" I spun away from him, wished there was something I could lash out against.

The old anger.

What would life be without it?

"Swearing like that," he said, "is the sign of a fucking tired mind."

I didn't say anything. Slowly turned back. Saw that he was grinning. Made me think of *Alice in Wonderland*, that Cheshire Cat.

"I'm tired of you and your fucking games." I felt

the urge to get in his face. Resisted. "I don't help you, so you break into my office? Sorry, you get some other poor prick to break in... because you think you're fucking entitled. That you're the fucking king of this city?"

He didn't respond straight away. Seemed to consider what I said for a moment. "I think... you need some rest."

I could have come up with a snappy response. Or walked away. I could have done a million things.

But what I did was snap.

Stepped forward, grabbed his shirt with one hand and slammed a swift fist into his kidneys with the other. He wasn't ready for it, made it easier for me to get the upper hand. He'd had his brawling days about ten years back. Sure, he still had muscle, but he was old and unprepared. I hauled him back against the rough brick wall of his house. His head rocked. The back of his skull smacked against brickwork.

He blinked a few times like the world had just gone out of focus.

I got in his face.

"You try another stunt like that again – I don't care if it's your fucking mother in trouble next time – and I'll kill you. I'll come here. Kill you." I eased up a little, stepped back. "You said last year I had that in me, the fucking killer instinct. You want to put that to the test? Aye?"

His eyes were unfocussed. He wasn't looking at me.

I thought, for a second, *concussion*.

And then realised, he was looking at someone behind me.

Slowly, I turned around.

109

Saw that his guests had come outside.

One of them was staring at me like he couldn't quite believe what he was seeing.

I stared back, probably mirrored his expression.

DCI Ernie Bright. In his civvies. A glass of wine in one hand. An unlit cigarette in the other.

Ernie fucking Bright.

Chapter 18

"Get it over with."

Ernie sighed, sat back and locked his hands behind his head. I might have called his expression one of fatherly concern, but maybe that was reading too much into things.

Wishful thinking.

I never thought about my parents.

A conscious decision?

Can't say I remember making it.

Ernie seemed about to say something and then stopped. Unlocked his hands and leaned forward.

Restless.

"I should do it, too. Arrest your arse. Charge you like the eejit you are."

"I wouldn't blame you."

"Things are more complicated than that."

"Really?"

I wasn't even going to ask what he was doing at Burns's house. Dressed up like he was over to the neighbours for dinner. Like the scheming old prick was a friend.

Deep cover?

Aye, believe that if it makes you feel better.

Ten, fifteen years ago it might have been close to the truth. These days, there was no excuse. The backroom deals the Scottish police made with high level gangsters in the late eighties and early nineties were legendary.

Unless...

But why would I believe that of the man I had called my mentor?

"Susan's worried about you."

I tried to shrug that off. "She always has been."

"She said you were making progress. Getting better."

"I wasn't ill."

Ernie chuckled. No real humour. "Sometimes we all wondered."

I leaned forward. Conspiratorial. "Tell me Ernie..." A whisper: "What the fuck are you doing here?"

He sat back. On the defensive. "We don't talk about that."

"No?"

"I take you in, it's because I was in the area and heard the commotion."

"Shite. You were a guest. At his house. Afternoon fucking tea?"

He took in a breath between gritted teeth. Looked ready to start shouting, but spoke softly when he said, "I told you, it's complicated."

Christ, I'd already made the insinuation, figured I might as well go all the way: "Something tells me it's not your superiors you're afraid of."

Hell of a punch. Check the shift in his expression, the way his eyes darted. Searching for the exit.

We were having a nice friendly chat in the upstairs spare room of Burns's house and not down at the station because Ernie didn't want his daughter to know that he'd been here. If not exactly sleeping with the enemy, then certainly drinking with him.

The question was why.

Keeping tabs on Burns?

Or something else?

I see-sawed between wanting to forgive Ernie and grabbing him by the collar, yelling about how I'd trusted him. How he'd been the kind of copper I fucking aspired to be when I was on the force.

In the end, I stayed stuck between both those options, just wanting to get out of there, head home and lock the damn door.

Sod the investigation.

Sod Wickes and his sob story.

Sod everything.

"So what happens, now?"

"You tell me you've calmed down. You apologise. You leave."

"Fuck that!" I was almost out the chair again.

"Calm down, McNee." Three words, spoken quietly, but with a power behind them that could have flattened a bus.

I sat back in the chair. Starting an incident here would be counterproductive at best.

Aye, check Mr fucking Calm.

Ernie said, "You know I worked deep with the old man in the 80's. Back room deals. All that shite."

I said, "But it pays not to..." There was no better phrase, bad as it sounded in the circumstances, "burn your bridges."

Ernie had led a raid on Burns's home a few years

back. I'd been part of the team. Remembered the frost between the two men. Like they knew each other but hadn't spoken in years.

An act? Oh, aye. A bloody brilliant one and all.

Ernie sighed. "You want me to arrest you?"

I said nothing.

"You want to apologise to the man? Make this easy on everyone? He'll accept it. Like nothing ever happened."

Again, I kept schtum. Figured if I couldn't knock Ernie's block off, I could make him sweat some at least.

There was just the two of us in the upstairs room. No sound except for the guests downstairs. Talking loud and drinking hard.

***

Burns said, "I didn't touch your office."

Did I believe him?

Did I shite.

Not that it mattered. I'd taken the safe road. Told Ernie I'd do the whole shake-hands gig and then get out.

Deal with the devil?

Better the one you know.

Across the other side of the wee office room, Burns waited patiently.

Looking around, you would think this was the office of any small businessman. A room in the house dedicated to files and folios and figures. You wouldn't guess at what this man did.

What he had done.

You'd look at the photograph of the man's son on the desk, never realise that the lad had left town

114

ashamed of his heritage, of what the old man had done to get him through accountancy school.

Burns was standing between me and the door, his hand outstretched. Not looking like a monster. Just a man waiting for his apology.

Christ, that thought alone killed me.

I said, "I'm sorry," tried not to wince as I stepped across and offered my hand.

Did I look like I meant it? No idea, but Burns seemed to buy into it. His grip was firm and his hands were hot, like he was burning up on the inside.

I hoped he was.

Hoped it hurt like hell.

***

Outside, I drove away from the house fast. My hands hurt from the tension, and I stopped a few streets away, drawing in fast and bumping the pavement with my tyres.

I dialled a number on the mobile. Dropped my head so my skull smacked the padded headrest.

I breathed out long and slow as the line beeped in my ear.

Susan answered: "Steed?"

I didn't say anything.

"What do you want?"

That churning in my gut again.

I pulled the phone away from my ear, hit the cancel button.

Lashed out with my fist on the dashboard rather than let loose the tears I could feel stupidly gathering in my eyes.

Second time that day.

Maybe the car was the problem.

Chapter 19

"So you're the Golden boy?"

We'd met each other a few times before. Never had much to say other than hello and goodbye. But I knew her name.

She only remembered mine after a couple minutes dancing around the subject. Why would she remember me, after all? A few nods as we passed each other in FHQ hallways? Hardly the stuff of a grand friendship.

I felt stupid being at the house, welcomed in like an old friend when I didn't deserve it. I was twenty-eight years old, barely felt out of school most days, and everyone here seemed so sure of themselves.

Even this constable who was two years my junior.

The gathering – not quite large enough to call it a party – had been Ernie's idea. An informal evening to introduce me to some of the guys from CID, soften them up to the idea of my transferring in once I passed the exams. There were a few other beat coppers as well, all looking for a leg up. None of them looking as lost as I felt.

They could play the game. They'd been waiting for this kind of opportunity their whole career. Politics as exciting to them as the work itself.

She said, "He won't shut up about you." Meaning her father. This girl, the reason I knew her name was that she was the DI's daughter. I had enough nous to try and remember those kinds of facts at least.

I smiled, took it for a joke, not a barb. Susan smiled back. I couldn't read her expression.

I wished Elaine wasn't away on some stupid conference trip. She'd have helped me here, given me a gentle nudge through the social minefield.

I said, "I'm not sure if that's a good thing."

Susan said, "He did mention that, of course." Nodding at me as though she'd noticed something.

"That what?"

"That seriousness. You walk around like you're carrying the weight of the world on your shoulders."

I tried to keep the grin going. Hard work. She was making me sweat.

She said, as though she'd been thinking about the matter for a while, "Not sure if it suits you."

I had no idea how to take her. Was she playing with me? Her idea of fun; exploiting people's insecurities? Maybe she was going to rat me out to her father as an arsehole.

My shirt stuck to my skin. Christ, could anyone see it?

Around us people talked with ease and familiarity. Those who had been strangers minutes earlier talked like they'd known each other for years. Inane discussions that sounded so easy coming from everyone else's lips. Casual handshakes. Big smiles. Effortless laughter.

And me in the middle of it all, sweating to make small talk with the host's daughter.

Would it have been easier if she wasn't a copper, too?

Maybe.

But I doubted it.

I was overcome with the overwhelming sensation that everyone could see me as a fake. A kid who wasn't ready to step up yet. They were asking themselves what was Ernie Bright thinking, marking this wee eejit for promotion and transfer?

Finally, knowing I'd fucked up completely, I went outside, sparked up a cigarette. I'd quit three months earlier. But Elaine wasn't with me, and maybe I deserved this one. For the endurance; getting through as much of the evening as I had without utterly pissing it up.

I became aware of someone watching me. Could feel their eyes focussed on my back. I turned, saw Susan standing just inside the French windows at the rear of the house.

She stepped out onto the patio with me. "You don't fit in."

"That obvious?"

"He said you were smart…"

I knew where she was going. "But not exactly sociable."

She smiled at that, came and stood beside me and looked up at the sky. The moon was at three quarters, slipping in and out from beneath the scudding clouds.

"It's a game," she said. "The social part. You don't have to mean what you say, just look like you do."

"That's not so easy."

"You wear your heart on your sleeve?"

I didn't know how to respond to that. Just turned to look at her. She nodded. "Aye, that you do."

"You think there's something wrong with that?"

"How would I know?"

I nodded, looked back at the sky.

"Seriously, if my dad's got a good feeling about you, it's nothing to be ashamed of."

"I'm not."

"Then go in there and prove him right."

"Huh?"

"I don't like to see him embarrassed. And that's what you're doing tonight. By not playing the game, you're making him look like a prat."

"What if I don't like the game?"

"Then suck it up." She casually flicked out a hand, knocked my cigarette from between my fingers. "Ask yourself where you want to be in five years time. And whether you really want to be there. Then you'll know whether you can play the game." She slipped her hand through my arm to pull me back inside. "I'll show you how it's done, pal. It's easy, believe me."

And I guess I did.

***

Five years after that party, I was alone. Not just professionally, either.

Elaine was long gone.

And there was no one else.

Right?

Sitting in the car, still fuming from the encounter with Ernie Bright, I took a deep breath, started the engine. Closed my eyes and saw Susan. Not as she was now, but as she had been at her father's party.

119

Cocky. Confident. But still young and inexperienced.

I'd been the same way, I guess. Just without that self-assurance to fool everyone around me.

I don't know that I ever found it, either.

Chapter 20

This was the sensible move:

Go to Susan and tell her everything. Admit the truth. Just deal with it. She was working the case, after all.

Sure, my experience with her father – the man in charge of the Furst investigation – complicated matters. But in the end, maybe the knowledge that someone knew his secret would only double his dedication to finding the girl.

Back on the induction courses I took with the Association of British Investigators, one of the instructors talked about our relationship with law enforcement:

"The police are not our enemy. Forget all this crap about being Britain's second police force. There are limits to our skills. Our powers. There is no such thing as carte-blanche for an investigator. We have to know when to step back. When to say no. When to see that our clients are asking us to act outside the law. When to know that we ourselves are acting unlawfully, no matter how justified we believe our reasons to be."

And more:

"An investigator is not a vigilante. An investigator is not an outlaw. He is a professional with a distinct sphere of influence. There are clearly defined edges to any case. We do not blur the lines. We do not lose ourselves in heroic fantasies or self-aggrandizing bollocks."

In other words, we know when to quit.

I pulled my mobile, made to dial Susan's number, but hesitated with my thumb over the call button.

We do not blur the lines.

I put the phone back down.

Wickes talked a good game. And I felt for him; his need to try and put right his own mistakes.

I could help him find the redemption he was looking for. It didn't have to take me or him outside of the law to do that. Once we found out the truth, we called in the professionals.

And Wickes had said as much himself, men like us were uniquely placed to slip into the places the police could never go.

Heroic fantasy?

Self aggrandizing bollocks?

Maybe.

I dialled in another number.

Wickes answered in three rings.

I said, "You went to the school?"

"Got nothing."

"All the same, I think someone's bound to know something."

"I have some leads," he said. "A few things I could check out. Places she used to go. People she knew."

"I want to give the school another shot," I said. "They knew Mary and they knew Deborah. I don't know, maybe someone there knows something."

"They don't," he said. "She wasn't social. Wouldn't have mixed with her fellow teachers. They'll tell you what I already know, that she was a recluse. Kept herself to herself. Probably appeared aloof to everyone. Nobody really knew her."

"Sometimes," I said, "It just takes asking the right question."

Wickes was silent. Finally, he just hung up on the line.

I didn't call back. Figured he was under enough pressure.

That was all.

Chapter 21

For all the shite Dundee takes from the rest of Scotland– a folk-reputation for violence, thuggery, idiocy and poverty – it has some of the best schools in the country. Dundee High is a private school with a national reputation, and the public schools do pretty good for themselves as well.

I knew a few kids who went to Bellview – in the North West of the city – when I was younger. Over a decade and a half since I'd graduated, and yet when I pulled up outside the main building, it was as though nothing had changed. The buildings were exactly the same, but then, what had I expected?

The campus was centred on an old, imposing Victorian building. The received wisdom of Dundee school pupils is that Bellview used to be a mental hospital. What we'd charmingly call the nuthouse, the loonybin. Anything to make it sound more frivolous than it was.

You have to love the ingrained Scots' attitude to mental health. Find yourself in anything less than perfect condition – and admitting to it – you're seen as "a bit soft". Or, *touched* as my gran used to say.

I never found out if that particular rumour about the asylum was true, but it still made sense to me when I saw the serious nature of the architecture and the imposing grandeur of the brickwork on the main building.

I left the car in the visitor's car park, walked up the main doors. Signs said, *Visitors this way,* and warned about being thrown off school property without the correct identification.

Back when I was at school, you could wander the halls with impunity. These days, everyone was scared. Sometimes you had to wonder whether the world was really a more violent place or whether we made it so by constantly acknowledging our social fears and insecurities.

I followed the signs, found the office. I rapped the safety glass, got the attention of a blonde lass who didn't look like she was long out of the school herself.

"Help you?"

"I'd like to talk to the rector." I didn't have a name, but it seemed like an idea to go straight to the top. When in doubt, just looking like you know what you're doing can work wonders.

"You have an appointment?"

I shook my head. Bashful smile. Figured it might work with this girl. "No. I'm…" Fumbling in my pockets, I pulled out my wallet and my ABI membership; closest thing to a license for the UK, although a change was whispering in on the breeze. The Security Industry had changed a great deal in the new millennium, with smaller, independent operators feeling the worst squeezes. Belonging to an organisation like ABI took some of the pressure off.

I said to the girl behind the glass, "I'm an investigator. I need to talk to the rector about –"

She got it before I finished. "You can talk to the police about Mary Furst." She'd probably already had enough pricks trying to get in on the story over the last forty-eight hours. I wasn't of any interest to her now; just another ghoulish prick looking for scandal.

I said, "I'm not here to waste anyone's time."

"I said, no."

I thought of old public information campaigns: *No means no.*

The blonde girl, raised her eyebrow. Looked a little like a female Mr Spock from the old *Star Trek*.

I returned the look. If rational argument wouldn't work out, then maybe the stubborn arsehole approach might achieve something.

What do they say about desperate times?

She caved first.

Told me, "Wait here."

I waited till her back was turned before I relaxed. Felt a little smile creep about my face. Killed it fast.

She made a call from a phone near the back of the office. Keeping her voice low so I couldn't hear anything. Kept turning her gaze back to me as though afraid I'd maybe bolt.

Wouldn't have made her day any worse, I reckoned. But I stayed where I was.

The girl finished on the phone, but didn't come back to the glass.

Further down the corridor, a door opened.

The woman who walked out was in her mid thirties, tall and slim, with a sober, no-nonsense dress sense. Dark-red hair fell in ringlets down her back,

126

and while her features were soft, she had eyes that burned with intensity. Guess they were the kind of eyes a good teacher needed, could stare down the most belligerent of pupils. I certainly felt a little unnerved, half-expecting her to accuse me of skipping class. She wore a trouser suit with a silk blouse that sat loosely on her frame.

"I'm Ms Foster," pronouncing the Mizz clearly. But I could see the wedding band on her finger. "You're the second investigator I've talked to today."

***

Ms Foster was cut out for the teaching life. Had the look down cold. The one that made you feel guilty even if you hadn't done anything yet.

I was sweating hard.

Hadn't even sat down.

The rector's office.

Christ, some aspects of childhood never quite escape us.

I waited for the invite. Playing the game carefully. She knew I wanted something, wanted to know what it was and even then didn't want to give it to me.

Christ, all I wanted was some clue as to what happened to Mary Furst.

The girl had been missing over 24 hours now.

The coppers would be searching for a corpse soon.

"You want to tell me why you're here?"

I said it fast and firm: "Mary Furst."

"You and everyone else in the country"

I said, "Tell me about her art teacher."

Like a slap across the face. Oh, aye, check that

127

highly visible reaction. Her face reddened. Her eyes darted away from contact with mine. Her hands reached to grip the desk in front of her.

Steady, now.

I said, "They were close. The girl and her teacher. Not quite what you'd expect."

"Who told you?"

"An investigator listens to what's going on around him."

"You're not like the other one."

The other one?

She second guessed me, said, "The other investigator."

"No," I said. "I'm not."

"All the subtlety of a natural disaster."

I nodded. Definitely Wickes.

"Had him ejected from the premises."

I wanted to ask, *why*, but figured it would only lead to questions about why I wanted to know. And then how I knew Wickes. He made that bad an impression on Ms Foster, I didn't want her connecting us. It would only sever what was already a tenuous relationship.

Investigations are built on relationships.

This business, it's all about people.

I said, "Tell me about the teacher. About Deborah Brown."

Ms Foster chewed on her lower lip.

I prompted: "Mary had an interesting family."

"The private affairs of –"

"Her godfather is a known criminal."

"Never arrested. Never proven. A businessman, Mr McNee." Did she believe it? Like hell.

All the same, I nodded. Like I understood her. Like I agreed.

128

She said, "And what does that have to do with Miss Brown?"

"They were close, Mary and... Miss Brown," I said. "I know that. Maybe even know why. And here's the thing, Ms Foster." I placed the emphasis on her title, calling her on the pretentiousness of it. "I want to find Mary. I think the police are looking in all the wrong places."

It wasn't quite enough.

I leaned forward, caught her eyes so she couldn't turn away. "I know you have a reputation to protect. I know you're conflicted about protecting your staff and admitting the truth. In here, it's just you and me talking. None of it leaves this room."

I meant it, too.

And I think for a moment her guard dropped. And she understood me.

We made the connection.

The connection that means everything for an investigator.

Chapter 22

Sometimes I feel as though my life is made up of other people's stories.

Do I have any perspective on my own affairs when I spend so much time entrenched in other people's?

I'm not sure if I would want an answer to that.

"Some pupils are talented with numbers or language," Ms Foster told me. "Very few are truly talented artists. Not in the way that Mary was... is." She ran a hand through her long hair. Uncomfortable, maybe wondering just how much she should be telling and what she should be keeping back.

"She came to your attention?"

Ms Foster allowed herself to smile. "You try to keep in touch with what's going on... out on..." she hesitated, as though choosing her words carefully, before saying, "the front lines." She shot me a nervous grin, as though checking I was in on what was clearly a joke shared among the teachers. "Some pupils float to the top of the pile. Sometimes for the wrong reasons." She made sure I caught the eye contact this time. The firm seriousness in her face. "But not with Mary."

"Her mother told me, she's a model pupil." I was careful to avoid slipping in past tense, no matter how accidentally.

"Aye, I guess if there is such a thing. Like I said, talented. And smart. Her test scores were... impressive. We were guessing A's by the end of her higher exams."

"You knew her to talk to?"

Ms Foster nodded. "Like I said, I try to keep in touch. Try and meet as many pupils face to face as I can. She was assured, you know."

I sensed something else.

Didn't tease it out.

Just waited.

Let Ms Foster interrogate herself. Sometimes all you have to do is sit back and listen.

She gave a little cough, as though clearing her throat. Passed a hand delicately in front of her mouth. "I mean, for a teenager. The thing... I mean, I don't... she was confident, and the staff adored her, and so did most of her peers, but..."

I had to push. Just a little.

Call it a nudge.

"... Sometimes she'd drop off during class, I guess. Drift, I mean. She wouldn't quite be there. I mean, you asked her a question, she'd answer it, but I think it unnerved a couple of the more demanding teachers." She smiled again, too broadly for it to be comfortable. "I still teach a few lessons. Keep my hand in. A few Soc-ed – that's Social Education – classes on the timetable so that I can keep in touch with the pupils. I've witnessed it myself, this sudden distance that would come over her."

"Don't most kids have a short attention span?"

131

She nodded, smiled. "Of course. I don't even know why I mentioned it."

Neither did I. But there was a reason, somewhere.

"She never had any troubles at home?"

"Not that I knew."

"And you say… her peers… her classmates… they all liked her?"

"Yes. Like I said, I didn't know of –"

"What about Richie Harisson?"

That made her pause. She lifted her head. "What about him?"

"They were going out, right?"

She licked her lips. A quick, darting motion. "I don't see –"

"The police must have asked already. I'm not asking for anything you didn't tell them."

She took a breath. "I don't know about that."

"You know something."

"Like I said, I knew her. She stood out. For her talent. For her attitude. For being in the drama society, volunteering on the paired reading programme with the younger kids, all of that. But that doesn't mean I knew anything about her life. Not outside of –" She cut herself off. Maybe regretting the fact that when asked she knew only facts about this girl who had gone missing, but had nothing to say about Mary as a person that was definitive and utterly personal.

What had I expected from her, of course?

I said, "Maybe you didn't know her. But you knew Deborah Brown."

And she did. Didn't have to say a word to tell me that.

132

Chapter 23

"She was extremely open in interview," Ms Foster told me. "More than anyone I'd ever met. Normally, I'd find it unsettling, but she was one of those people who made you feel like they were your best friend." She smiled, a reflex reaction that she quickly retracted. "I don't know how to explain it. She had the same effect on everyone. Including Mary."

I said, "Tell me about her."

"What do you mean?"

"Family. Friends. Lovers. What she liked to do in the evening."

"She... I mean... I know she got her degree at Glasgow College of Art. I know... I know..."

I sat back.

Figured as much. Some personality types are social magicians. They distract you with empathy, give you nothing in return and you don't even realise. Most of these people are simply private. But some of them...

"When did you start to get suspicious?" I asked.

"I never said –"

"You didn't have to."

Ms Foster shifted again. Ran a hand through her hair in a gesture without confidence that made me think of a nervous teenage girl trying to hide what she felt. In this room she would normally have the balance of power on her side. Dealing with pupils. Other members of staff. People she could control. No wonder she'd been hesitant to speak to me. I was an unknown quantity.

She said, "It's that obvious?"

I nodded.

Her head bowed a little so that her long hair fell across her face. She pushed against the desk and stood up. Walked to the large windows and looked outside.

"Did she have any friends?" I asked.

"People tried. Like I said, she was open and honest. But..."

"She didn't socialise."

"No."

"Boyfriends?"

"None that I knew of. Once, we had dinner together. My attempt to get to know her better. I took her... we went to that place on Brook Street... named after the jazz player."

I knew the place. "Beiderbeckes."

Ms Foster nodded. "She seemed to open up a little, and I thought maybe everything would be okay, that she was just thrown by being thrust into this new environment." Ms Foster kept her back to me as she talked. Seemed to be focussing on something in the distance, out on the horizon. "She told me about a boyfriend she had in Glasgow. How she had come here to escape him."

"Escape?"

She spun on her heels to face me. "That's the word she used."

"She say why?"

"Not really. The minute she told me, she seemed to realise what she'd said and tried to switch the subject. I let her. I was her boss, you know? We weren't that close. I guess I realised it after that lunch."

I nodded.

Something wasn't sitting right.

"What about her family? I mean, did she ever talk about having –"

"She said she had a sister."

"A daughter?"

Ms Roger's brow furrowed. She took a step towards me. "She didn't have any children. None that she mentioned."

"You look concerned," I said.

"Just something someone said." She let her face relax, and leaned back against the sill of the large window. Looking almost at ease. Her defences down, as though she'd forgotten all her initial antagonism towards me.

A good sign from my point of view.

Her head had tilted back. She wasn't looking at me any more. "They said, seeing her and Mary together, sometimes they looked more like mother and daughter than teacher and pupil." She smiled. "Silly, really. Or it was at the time."

She stood up again. Looked at me strangely, her head tilted to one side. "Who did you say you were again?"

"I'm an ex-copper. Used to work alongside Detective Bright."

She kept her back to me. "The man in charge?"

Stretching the truth? Just a little. I played it cool, said, "That's the one."

"And you're working with him now? In some kind of advisory capacity?"

I nodded. Kept up the eye contact. Kept her in tune with me. No hesitation. No uncertainty. She had to believe I was telling her the truth.

One of the most powerful weapons in your arsenal – as an investigator, working for the police or for a private client – is the way you use words. Most of the time you can deal with anyone if you know the words or the tones that will persuade them to co-operate with you.

You need to be as sneaky as a con artist.

Finally, she said, "It's not unusual for a teacher to take interest in a particularly bright or talented pupil. You think someone can do well, you want to encourage that. Rewards of the profession, you know? Christ knows there are few enough of those these days."

I nodded. Said nothing. Silence can be as big a motivator during interview as anything else.

"It was only later… people began to talk."

"Talk?"

"They were seen together outside school a lot. Not unusual, I guess, when the kids get older. They start to show more interest, sometimes the teacher takes on more of a mentor role."

"But other times –"

"Other times there's talk."

"Not just about them looking like mother and daughter."

Ms Foster sighed, deeply. "The tabloid press like their scandals. I'll tell you straight up, Mr McNee, that the actual number of affairs between teachers

136

and pupils is very small." Was she quick on the defensive? Maybe, but I got the feeling she'd heard the insinuation more than enough times over the past couple of days. Probably the past couple of months from the way she was speaking. "Normally, as well, it happens between members of the opposite sex. Statistically, I mean."

I didn't bother to tell her that I wasn't thinking that way. That I knew the truth. That it was maybe even stranger than she suspected.

She kept talking. She'd started this thing, was going to finish it. "I didn't think the talk, the rumour mill, was founded on anything." Another pause. Another reluctant admission: "She used to invite Mary over to her place. Never any of the other pupils. It was... unusual."

"More than favouritism?"

That put her back on edge. "I don't want to draw conclusions." Aye, she could talk the talk, but she'd had doubts of her own.

"Why didn't you tell the police about this?"

"I did... but they didn't seem... they didn't ask any further."

They didn't? Surprised me. But not if they were holding back information. Susan had been cagey when I mentioned Deborah's name earlier.

Aye, according to our arrangement. I was an observer. But they were hiding things from me. Putting the blinkers on.

Maybe more so since my little encounter with Ernie.

"What did they ask about?"

"You're working with them, right?"

One wrong question. I lost her.

Easy to do. Takes one wrong turn and you pull

137

someone straight out of what they're saying, remind them they need to keep their guard up.

I'd slipped up, indulging my personal curiosity. Trying to find out what facts had been hidden from me and why, when I should have been continuing to show concern for the girl.

Mary Furst should have been all that should have mattered.

Ms Foster said, "Maybe I should call the DCI?" Her tone was clipped. Authoritarian. She had her power back.

I nodded, said, "I'm not sure there's anything else you can tell me for now."

"All the same –"

"All the same, I should be going. Case like this, it's time sensitive."

"McNee," she said. "That was your name, right?"

I stood up. Feeling my face burn. My heart hammer.

Fuck.

I'd told Susan I wouldn't get too deep into this case. That I was *observation only*. She'd known from the start I was talking shite.

Knew me better than I knew myself, the way that old cliché goes.

I started to back away.

Ms Foster kept her gaze fixed on me.

I left the room, made a quick walk down the corridor.

Feeling like the worst kind of eejit.

Chapter 24

Back in the car, I called Wickes on the mobile number he'd given me.

He answered in three rings.

"My partner in crime," he said. Laughed. The same animal sound I'd heard from him earlier. It made me uneasy for some reason. I couldn't quite put my finger on it.

Not in the mood for jokes, I said, "Where are you?"

He gave me an address. His tone suddenly formal. I'd upset him with my own straight-to-business routine. He'd get over it.

I said, "Is that supposed to mean something?"

"Grumpy bastard this afternoon, aren't you? I tracked Deborah down. A flat registered in her sister's name. I checked it out as far as I could. The sister doesn't live there. She's keeping an empty home. Strike you as suspicious? Right now I'm supposed to be meeting with the landlord."

"No one's home?"

"You think she would be?"

"Have you talked to the sister?"

"You seriously think she'd talk to me? I told you what happened when we met before. As far as she's concerned I'm the bloody devil. Price you pay for trying to do the right thing, aye?" Painting himself as the martyr. And maybe he was.

But for all I wanted to like him, the more I listened to him talk, the more I felt that he was lying to me. Hiding the truth.

From himself as much as me.

I said, "If you have a line on the sist –"

"You think she'll tell us anything?" Mocking me. The kind of verbal whip that gives you pause for thought.

"I want you to be sure," I said. "I want you to be sure that Deborah's in that flat. Then we call the cops, and they deal with –"

"No. No fucking way, McNee. You can't do that to me." A rush to his words. I couldn't tell if he was scared or just plain angry.

I was thinking about my meeting with Ms Foster at Bellview. Her mentioning the other investigator. She hadn't described him to me, but I knew it had been Wickes.

He told me he'd been there. But he hadn't made a grand impression. They'd chucked him out on his arse. The question was why?

Stopping to think about it, what did I know about this man?

He was a fellow investigator.

With no references. No affiliations. Nothing to back up his story except old war stories about his career and the kind of earnest grin that made you want to believe him.

Where had he heard of me? He never really said. Talked about my reputation, but never gave any specifics.

Who the fuck was this guy?

"We need to talk to the police," I said. "I know the investigating officers. They're good people…" Well, one of them at least. The one who wasn't jumping into bed with known figures in organised crime.

"You mean DCI Ernie Bright?" Wickes said, and I could hear a chuckle rumbling beneath the question.

"Aye."

"You know his history? He was one of the officers offered David Burns a deal in the nineties. Worked with that bawbag to cut some kind of immunity in exchange for bringing down other gangs and known dealers. Christ, I wouldn't trust that crooked bastard as far as I could throw him."

I tried to muster some belief into my voice. "That was a long time ago. That program was sanctioned by the police, ended when they realised that it was doing more harm than good."

"So he was following orders? He told you all about it?"

I swallowed. "Yes." I could pass this one on a polygraph, right?

Wickes was silent.

I could figure his reluctance. This investigation wasn't about finding Mary for him. This was about Deborah. This was about confronting her. Asking her why, after all he had done for her, she still betrayed him.

Did I understand his obsession?

His self-delusion?

Maybe.

You love someone, you wind up doing stupid things. Losing your sense of perspective. Your world revolves around the object of your love.

You end up sacrificing yourself for them.

I figured this was why he and Deborah had found themselves together; some recognition of one for the other.

Each was obsessed.

Wickes with Deborah.

Deborah with the daughter she never knew.

I said, into the phone, "There are other leads on what might have happened to Mary." Meaning the ex-boyfriend. Meaning she could have simply run off. I wanted Wickes to start thinking rationally about all of this: "You want to check out this place? When you don't know for sure –"

"Aye, and what have you been doing, pal? The way you were talking earlier, sounded like personal business."

"I was at the school," I said. Held a second to listen for some kind of reaction. Maybe a giveaway about what he'd been doing there before me. But all I got was the steady sound of his breathing. "And I was going to go have a wee chat with Mary's boyfriend. Have to admit, I was running the investigation, he'd probably be my first choice of suspect."

"You wouldn't be holding anything out on me, pal?" Wickes asked it blunt. No slyness involved. Nothing that sounded like suspicion.

"No," I said. Unsure whether it really was a lie. "I just want to make sure we're not overlooking any possibilities."

I arranged to meet him later, we'd see where his lead with the flat went.

After I hung up, I put the phone down on the passenger seat. Feeling lightheaded.

This was a bad idea. I knew it. Understood it. And still...

142

I should have called Susan. Ended the whole sorry affair right then.

But I had to know about Wickes. His stakes in all of this. He was hiding something; I knew it then: was absolutely convinced of it. He had lied to me. That was what stung the most.

Injured pride?

Aye, that and I was curious. Needed to know. To understand. Once I had some answers, could make sense of this man and his obsession with finding the missing girl and the woman he claimed was her mother, then I could go to Susan. Tell her everything.

If I went any earlier, I'd lose my chance. Maybe never be able to make sense of anything that had happened.

Talk about that itch you can't scratch.

Chapter 25

Dundee was Scotland's fourth city in terms of size, constantly jockeying with Aberdeen for the coveted position of third. But its reputation as the city with the small town feel was what gave it the edge. Stay there long enough, you felt like you knew the streets and the people intimately.

One of the strange contrasts of the city came in the way that neighbourhoods were spread out. Poverty sat on the doorstep of middle class comfort without anyone batting an eyelid. There were no ghettos, just a few wrong turns.

Which is why Richie Harisson's parent's comfortable, mid-sized bungalow sat in the shadow of old council tower blocks that cast a jealous shadow across their neighbours.

I pulled up and idled for a few minutes on the main road outside. It was just past four, and most of my afternoon had been wasted at Burns' house and the school. Before driving over, I'd called Susan to ask if there had been a break in the case. Anything I needed to know.

She hadn't answered.

I hadn't left a voicemail.

Walking up the path to the front door, I felt a chill in the air and couldn't figure whether the temperature was dropping or I was suffering some kind of psychosomatic reaction.

Did it matter?

I chapped the front door three times. Rapid. Hard. Waited.

The woman who answered was small, with blonde hair cropped short, and blue eyes enveloped by bags that had clearly come with the years. She was dressed in a cheap looking blouse and dark trousers, wore chunky heels to give her that extra little bit of height. Even then, she barely passed five feet. I figured her age for early fifties at a kindly estimate.

"Aye?"

"Mrs Harrison?"

She nodded, wary.

"My name's McNee." I presented my card. She turned it over a few times as though looking for a hidden message. "I need to talk to your son."

"The police have been here."

"DCI Bright, right?"

She hesitated. "Said she was a DC."

At least I got the name right. But I figured I could stretch the truth a little. Mrs Harrison didn't strike me so sharp as Ms Foster had at the school. "I'm consulting with the official investigation."

"No one mentioned you."

"You can phone the detective in charge if you like." She looked as though she barely had the energy to pick up the receiver, never mind dial the digits.

"Aye, well," she said. "The lad's not here, anyway.

Fed up with all these eejits coming round, asking him about Mary. Hard enough on him and all that. If you do see him, Mr McNee, though, you can tell him he's getting a skelp behind the ear for cutting out. He should be at home with me. Where I can protect him."

I pulled out a card. Said, "Give Richie this. He wants to talk, he can."

She looked at the card. Said, "Who're you trying to fool? Nobody's a private investigator. Not in Dundee of all places."

I shrugged and stepped back. No point in forcing this one. She didn't want to talk. She wouldn't talk.

She wouldn't give me her son. Perhaps afraid of the questions I wanted to ask. The truths I might uncover.

Richie's mother closed the door in my face. Hard. I stood there for a moment, feeling somehow stunned. Then shook my head and turned to walk back out to the road.

I was about to get into the car when a voice said, "You're not the police."

I looked up and saw a lad sitting on the wall a few metres down he road. Doc Marten's, frayed jeans, attitude to spare. He looked at me from beneath a sandy fringe and his eyes had the attitude of the rebellious teenager.

He wasn't practised, though.

Likely, he'd perfected this act over the last few days. A defence mechanism.

I said, "Richie?"

"Aye. And who're you?"

"I'm consulting with the police."

He didn't question that. Just nodded and said, "Told that woman I didn't have anything to do with Mary."

146

That woman. Figured he meant Susan.

He hopped off the wall. "What do you mean you're 'consulting' with the police?" Smart kid, cutting straight through my crap.

"Just that. I'm an investigator."

"Aye?"

"Private."

"That's only from films."

I shook my head. "The real deal."

He laughed at that, got down off the wall and walked over to the car. Said, "Got a cigarette?"

"Bad habit."

He nodded. Said, "How'd you quit?"

"Willpower," I said. "The woman copper. Her name's Susan Bright. We're friends. She's the one asked me to dig a little deeper."

"I've got nothing else to say. So why'd they send you?" He shook his head, started to back off. "They think I did something to Mary."

"Did you?"

He nodded, made to walk off again. I followed. Caught up with him. He didn't seem to care, turned off the main road and took the gap between two houses. Heading to the old tower blocks.

I said, "You split up with Mary a few months ago?"

"Aye."

I leaned forward. "Hurts, right?"

He shrugged. "What do you care?"

I tried for a smile. "Hurts like a bastard. I know it. Really."

"The breakup? Aye... It was... mutual."

"Tell me," I said.

"She was... she wasn't interested any more."

"She tell you why?"

Didn't get a response. We kept walking up near

147

the high-rises, through patches of grassland that might have once been decorative but were now strewn with discarded glass and rubbish. There was no one around; from just beyond the buildings came the sound of traffic on the Lochee Road heading up towards Camperdown way.

I looked up at the high-rises. Social and architectural failures in every sense. The grand experiment, and it all got fucked up. Story of every city, I suppose, and it could have been worse. Dundee had a history to fall back on.

Some Scottish towns were built on nothing but experiments like this from back in the sixties, and were now something of a national embarrassment; synonymous in the popular public imagination with poverty and crime. A self-fulfilling prejudice.

Richie wasn't a high-rise kid. But I figured he kind of liked hanging around the buildings. He walked here with an ease I'd never have had at his age.

Mind you, it was still daylight and the open spaces seemed deserted. A ghost scheme.

He said, finally, "It was Ms Brown."

Deborah.

"What, it was her fault that you and Mary broke up?"

"Aye."

I wished that Wickes had really taken me on some kind of wild goose chase. Would have made my life simpler.

I didn't want his truths confirmed.

But I couldn't run from them either.

Richie stopped walking, looked at some graffiti on the side of one of the rises. Multi-coloured scrawls that didn't mean anything beyond boredom and anger.

I said, "Tell me."

He kicked at the wall. His manner sulky and awkwardly defiant. Aye, for all that attitude in his clothing and slouched shoulders, he was still little more than a boy. Didn't really know how to defend himself in this world.

Then again, do any of us?

***

Typical teenage romance.

Finding they were pushed together by mutual friends after cautious flirting. Deciding, *what the fuck*, and discovering they clicked.

For maybe... four or five months?

There are two types of teenage love that I remember. Theirs was the one I was most familiar with. The other one only seemed to happen to other people; the true *highschool sweethearts* who hooked up fourth or fifth year and remained sickeningly attached even when they headed off to university.

Maybe Richie and Mary would have wound up that way.

But Mary changed.

At least, the way Richie told it she did, "Pretty soon after Ms Brown took her for art."

Go figure.

"I don't know if... I mean, she started not being there. All the time, that is. Kept telling me how she couldn't be distracted. She wanted to be an artist. She was good, too. And she told me how I was dragging her away from that, how we didn't

149

need to spend every waking hour together." No bitterness there. Or no more than you'd expect from a teenage boy, anyway. "She told me how it was tough to be an artist and how she needed to spend so much time doing it and, well, I was fine with that except..." He still wasn't sure about what he was going to say next. I figured he knew that it could sound petty and jealous to the wrong ears. All appearances aside, I got the feeling Richie was a pretty sensitive kid, knew that he'd have been stupid to make his girlfriend choose between him and her dreams. "We never saw each other at all after a while. She spent all her time... not with me, anyway."

From what little I knew of Mary, she was smart, focussed and driven. Everything that Richie told me confirmed that. When he talked about her, his body language became fluid and expressive. He sat forward.

He told me how she used to hum to herself when she was working or reading. A habit she tried to break in time for exams, when silence in the hall was mandatory. And that she always wore a cross even though she told people she was a devout atheist. "She wore it because her godfather gave it to her."

For the breakup being mutual, it was clear he still carried a torch for her.

Don't we all when it comes to our first loves?

More and more the excuses came to be expected. He'd make a date, she'd agree, and then a call or text would break the arrangement off at the last minute. "Every time," Richie said, "she was with Ms Brown. Always. Everyone knew it, too, that she was spending more time with her art teacher than me."

He started kicking up dirt from the ground, staring at the toes of his boots. Spoke quietly; "Some people said things."

The rumours that Ms Foster had inferred.

The kind of whispers that could lose a teacher her job.

I had the feeling that Deborah Brown hadn't made a move to nip those in the bud. Probably hadn't even noticed they were circulating. No, all she would have cared about was not being close to her daughter again.

"I didn't want to believe them."

"Did you talk to her about it?"

He didn't say anything.

I said, "Did you want to talk to her about it?"

More silence. Aye, check the Scottish male: *let's not talk about this*.

"I told the police –"

"I don't care what you told them."

He looked ready to walk. But he wanted to tell me. I knew it. He just needed the right encouragement.

"Richie," I said, "We need to find Mary. You want to know what happened to her, same as me. You want to know she's all right. And believe me, pal, anything you can tell me… it's going to help. Even if it seems stupid."

He ran his hand through his hair, tugging as though to pull it out by the roots. His features squeezed tight, and I saw tears leak from the corner of his eyes. "I thought she was playing with me," he said. "Really, just messing with my head." He let his hands drop and his body relaxed completely. "When she told me about Ms Brown. I mean, that's why I didn't tell the police what she said. Because… it

151

wasn't true."

"What wasn't true?"

"She told me… told me Ms Brown… was her mum."

***

When I got back to the car, it was nearly four in the afternoon.

I was strangely light headed. Still couldn't figure why Deborah had abducted Mary. She'd been at the school for months. Working her way into the girl's affections.

Was this not enough?

And if Mary knew Deborah was her real mother, why the need for any of this?

What really unnerved me was the way everything seemed to jar with Wickes's story, even in subtle ways. All his talk of solidarity among people in our line of work was just so much smoke up my arse.

The sheer planning and patience involved with Deborah's plan seemed at odds with the impulsive and obsessive behaviour Wickes had described to me. I couldn't figure it.

And his own investigation seemed to have been delayed for reasons I couldn't understand. Why didn't he notice her odd behaviour sooner? Why not confront the sister straight away? Or even Burns?

So I was stuck questioning everything. Wondering what the hell was going on. And unable to leave it alone because pride dictated that I had to get to the bottom of it all. That I couldn't ask for help.

That I couldn't admit defeat.

Chapter 26

Jam.

Jute.

Journalism.

The three J's.

Every Dundonian kid was taught about them in history class. Every university student lectured on it during their orientation. The three J's were the lifeblood and heritage of Dundee.

Except they weren't the three J's because that first one was really an M. Marmalade. But, like the three R's of education, the three J's stuck because they sounded right.

Journalism still thrived. DC Thompsons remained a driving force in the UK publishing industry. *The Courier*, *The Sunday Post* and even *The Evening Telegraph* remained key in Scottish reporting. They produced some great journalists who went onto bigger and better things, and they were the publishers of Scotland's only surviving comics in *The Beano* and *The Dandy*.

The other J's had died.

Marmalade dried up fast.

Jute just about killed the city.

As demand for the threads diminished, whole factories came crashing to a close. The industry that had kept an entire city functioning left Dundee without jobs and its slow death crippled thousands of families.

For decades, the old mills stood empty. Waiting for...

Rejuvenation.

When it came, the rebirth manifested itself not as new industry but as apartment blocks and city centre pads for students and young professionals. The old mills found themselves gutted, given a new lease on life.

Check the stone building I pulled up in front of, with the new double glazed windows and the blue security doors anachronistically set into the heavy stonework.

Wickes was outside. Waiting with a skinny, dark-haired man whose shirt and trousers hung loosely on his frame, like all the clothes he could find were a little too large for him. He had an open face, what you might call trusting; the kind of innocent grin that made you warm to him fast.

Wickes said, "This is Timothy Stephen, owns Ms Brown's flat." He nodded at me and said, "My associate, Mr McNee."

Stephen said, "No first name?"

Wickes said, "I think he's embarrassed by it."

Stephen nodded, as though this explained everything.

I said, "Has my... associate... explained to you why we need to talk to Ms Brown?"

"Yeah... look... uh, this isn't... I mean, it's my dad

owns the place. I just… kind of… caretake, aye?"

I said, "You're responsible for the day to day upkeep of the building?"

"Sure. I deal with maintenance. Issues."

"Between tenants? Say, if someone was causing a problem…"

"Guess so. Aye." Stephen shuffled uncomfortably. Looked nervous, as though maybe he was expecting me and Wickes to start beating on him. Made me wonder how Wickes had made initial contact. "Look, uh… a question… this woman… what's she done?"

"It's old business," I said.

"This isn't going to cause trouble, is it?"

I shook my head.

Wickes clamped a heavy hand on Stephen's shoulder.

Neither gesture seemed to reassure the man.

They wouldn't have worked on me, either.

***

Deborah's flat was on the top floor.

She rented at £450 a month. One bedroom, although Stephen explained that for property reasons they called a second room a "study" area. "Can't call it a bedroom. No main window. Just a skylight. And it's small."

The inside of the converted mill was well maintained. Clean halls. Pot plants. Fresh paintwork. Coming through the main entrance, I'd seen a camera and Stephen had explained the entry buzzers provided a screen so you could see who was at the door.

We hadn't wanted to buzz up.

I wondered what Wickes had told this guy, he let

us in so easy.

Stephen said, "She's been a good tenant. Quiet. No trouble. Pays her bills on time." As though he was making excuses.

I looked at Wickes.

I'd ask him what he'd said later.

I said, trying not to sound out of breath from the stairs, "She pays in person?"

"Direct debit."

Somewhere around the fourth flight, I felt my left leg begin to burn. The muscles stretching, feeling ready to snap.

Psychosomatic?

Kiss my arse.

Deborah's door was nothing special. Off white, spyhole at eye-level.

What had I expected?

Stephen knocked at the door, announced himself. We waited.

Got nothing.

Two more attempts.

Stephen shrugged. "No one home."

Wickes said, "She's not coming back." Sounded ready to kick himself. He'd have to get in line behind me.

I was ready to give up. Say to Wickes, enough of this shite, let's just tell Susan what we know; let the coppers handle it.

Leave it to the professionals.

Before I had a chance to say anything, he jumped in: "We need inside. Maybe we'll find what we need."

Stephen raised his hands. "I can't let you in there. Unless you're with the police, forget it, pal."

"This is serious," said Wickes, his voice calm and measured. I listened hard for any kind of tremble, didn't get it. "A girl's safety is at stake."

Stephen stepped back, hands still raised. "This over my –"

Wickes moved fast. Deceptively so for a man his size. Reaching out, grabbing Stephen by his skinny shoulders and hurling him round so the man bounced against the wall.

"I'll use your head as a battering ram," Wickes roared, getting right in the other man's face. "I need to see inside the fucking flat, you little fucking tosser!"

I felt myself struggling to breathe. As though Wickes was getting in my face. I was paralysed. Not with fear so much as confusion.

Or the realisation that this side of Wickes had been there all along. I'd just been denying it. Trying not to notice.

We all like to think we're heroes, that when push comes to shove, we do the right thing. Step up and step in.

Aye, right.

What happened was, I froze.

Scared?

Maybe. Or just surprised, caught off balance by Wickes's outburst. A tactic? Had to be.

Stephen said, "I don't have the keys."

Wickes roared, and for a moment I thought he was about to make good on his threat. This time, I managed to step forward, reaching out with no idea what I was doing.

Was I going to attack the bastard?

Restrain him?

God help me, *help him*?

But it didn't matter, because his mood switched fast again. He let the skinny man drop and took a step back. Laughed that animal laugh of his and said, "We don't need keys. Just your permission, pal."

His *permission?*

Stephen was struggling to breathe, looked ready just to slide down the wall and collapse on the floor. He kept his eyes fixed on Wickes, maybe waiting for another assault. "Permission? *Fuck*, you've got it. OK? You've got it."

Wickes spun on his heels and winked at me. "Bet you couldn't do *that* as a copper, eh?" He was practically humming with energy. Like this was what he lived for.

I just nodded in a meek agreement. Still unsure he wasn't just playing some extreme game of good cop/bad cop.

If he was, it was a game he excelled at.

Chapter 27

Inside the flat, I was thinking: *walk. Just fucking walk, now.*

But I didn't.

What would have happened if I hadn't been there? How far would Wickes have gone?

I'd been having my doubts about him.

Nothing like this.

Stephen harped on about not having keys, but went quiet when Wickes gave him this look that could have flattened a village. I was tempted to ask where the big man learned his lock-picking skills, but given the situation I kept quiet.

Figuring I'd see where this was leading.

Remember what's important here: the girl's life.

Walking inside, I was overcome by a strange feeling of disappointment. *Is this it*? The flat consisted of, simply, an entrance hall with doors off. Kitchen. Bathroom. Bedroom. Living room. Spare room.

What did strike me was the sparse decoration.

No, not sparse.

Non-existent.

Wickes barged in through the front door like a bull. Stephen trotted behind, maybe worried about what damage the big man might cause. And not just to the flat.

I stayed in the doorway. Closed my eyes.

All of us acting like Wickes hadn't just made a threat on another man's life.

Wishful thinking can erase damn near anything.

The atmosphere was thick. Maybe my imagination. Or the situation. Either way I felt closed in and trapped.

For a supposedly rational man, I was acting spooked.

Trying to combat the sensation, I took my time; drinking in details and impressions. Keeping away from preconceptions and expectation. Letting the picture build.

Turning on my professional mind.

This was my case. Ignoring all personal conflicts with my client, I had a duty here. A need to remain detached.

I moved to the bedroom. Mattress on the floor. Nothing else. Not even carpeting.

The kitchen was empty.

No soaps in the bathroom. Ten to one bet the shower would run cold.

The living room: small TV and DVD player balanced on boxes. Couple of beanbags. No chairs.

The spare room was where things got interesting.

Wickes hadn't got there yet. Was messing with the DVD player in the living room, thinking he could get some clue from the latest rented blockbuster she'd left stuck in the machine.

Good.

I wanted the spare room to myself.

If Wickes had come in, he'd have run at the scene like a hurricane. Tearing everything down. Destroying anything useful that could be found.

I wouldn't have blamed him.

Not with what I saw.

The room was dark, the blinds dropped. Daylight seeped in cautiously as though frightened to illuminate what was scattered around on the floor and against the walls.

Canvases. Paints. Sketches.

Wickes had talked about Deborah's love of art. The way she saw the world, re-interpreted it through painting.

Maybe I began to understand the darkness he had talked about as well.

Images of rotting and darkened landscapes; urban and country, with dark skies and broken buildings. Waters raging as though boiling deep beneath the surface.

And through every image: the constant.

The motif.

A figure, lost and lonely. Always the same. Sometimes the dress shifting, but I realised – even when we saw her from a distance – that it was always the same girl. Her features were hidden in the rough style of the painter's brush, but as I started to piece everything together, my stomach lurched uncomfortably.

I recognised her.

The girl in the pictures. When she was turned to face the artist, with that half smile and her face partially hidden by hair that draped down across her features. I knew her. Even though we'd never met.

Mary Furst.

How many paintings – both those that were

finished and those that could be deemed works in progress – were in this room, stacked against the walls? I didn't want to count, but guessed around forty. All of them in that same, loose and destructive style: oils heavy and swirling darkly on the canvas. I started looking for a clear shot at the face, rifling the canvases, checking each image.

And I found it.

That face. In full profile.

Unmistakably *her*.

Painted with this expression of extreme sadness that pulled you into her eyes. No landscape on this one, just a head and shoulders portrait of a girl who looked every bit as broken as the landscape images that had preceded her. Her head was turned slightly to the side, her eyes downcast as though she didn't want to look at whoever was capturing this moment.

As though she was ashamed.

And it was the same girl, even if her manner was so different to the Mary Furst I had started to imagine through family photos and the talk of her friends and teachers. In these paintings she was not the perfect young lass with a future so bright it could blind, but someone more deeply conflicted than I could have guessed.

Wickes came into the room, saying, "You'll want to see –" The pictures drew him up short. "Bloody hell."

"Recognise any of these?"

He walked the walls, stopping in front of each image. Sometimes reaching out as though to touch the canvas, but pulling away at the last moment like something in the images unnerved him.

Make that two of us.

From the way his face pulled taut and from the

162

low growl that escaped his lips, I expected him to start screaming, punching the walls, breaking the frames. But instead he merely took a breath and turned to face me. Smiled awkwardly as if apologising for the outburst.

There was silence in the flat. The kind that comes before a storm.

Both of us were pretending like everything was good between us.

***

There was more, of course.

The DVD player. A disc inside. Home made. Shot on digital camera, transferred over.

Digital camera gives a cleaner picture than the old tape machines used to. But it doesn't mean you get a professional result into the bargain.

The film was jerky, unsteady, filmed by someone who didn't know the difference between viewing something with your own eyes and seeing it on a static screen.

I recognised the room straight away.

The lighting dull, the blinds drawn.

A girl was painting at an easel. Slow, delicate strokes, her back to the camera. Did she even realise she was being filmed? Hard to tell. Her body language was tight with concentration, but I didn't get the impression she was self-conscious about being filmed. Meaning a few things.

She was used to the idea of someone filming her.

Or she knew whoever was behind the camera.

Trusted them.

The girl had dark hair which she had tied back into a loose pony-tail. Hard to get a real idea of the colour in the half-light. Her neck was slender, and on the video her skin appeared supernaturally pale. She was dressed in a loose fitting dark jumper and light blue jeans.

I knew who she was.

Didn't want to admit it until she turned to face the camera.

It was strange to see her move.

I fought to suppress a shiver.

Had to convince myself this was not a dream.

The camera stayed on her face. Mary finally looked directly into the camera and in a moment of self-conscious realisation, she reached up to touch the cross that hung around her neck, the jewellery dark against her pale skin. She plied the necklace between her fingers, seemed to blush a little.

The cross around her neck, the gift from her godfather.

Looking at Wickes who stood beside me, I could see his skin paling. He turned to look at me. "That's the look she used to get," he said, and he was talking about Deborah. "When she was working. She looks like her, you know. Jesus fuck, it's uncanny."

We all carry something of our parents.

I carried some of my father's features. Not just outside, but also inside where I had inherited his doubts and anxieties. My mother used to say: *You're your father's son.* And I never knew whether her voice carried a hint of sadness in that.

I blinked.

Thought about Susan. Her father's angular face, her mother's gentle smile.

More and more I found myself thinking about her. My own feelings confused, as though that one night we had spent together was more than grief and sympathy confusing friendship for something else.

I blinked again. Forced the thoughts out of my head. Watched the images on screen.

Analysed. Considered.

Distracted myself.

Became the detective again. The investigator. The observer.

There was no sound on the film. Not a background hum or the thump of footsteps on naked floors. Nothing.

I watched Mary Furst's face, tried to see if her lips moved.

Watching that shaky camera work, I realised that we were seeing this girl through Deborah's eyes. This was how she saw the world. How she saw her daughter.

The focus was on the girl's face. We were watching her obsessively. Close enough to pick up on details. The camera never strayed out of focus. It moved with its subject. Entranced.

Wickes had mentioned obsession.

Was that what we were seeing?

I wasn't so sure. Having seen home movies before, I knew the way that parents often filmed their offspring with the same kind of intensity I was watching in front me.

Love.

Obsession.

Is there a difference?

Chapter 28

"He could have killed me."

"But he didn't."

I was out on the stairwell with Mr Stephen, the skinny man ready to get out his mobile, give the police a call.

Can't say I blamed him.

But I needed Wickes. His insight into Deborah for one thing.

The big man was holding back. He'd known this was a dead end, I was sure. But he'd wanted me to see the flat. The paintings. The home movie.

Why?

To convince me even further that Deborah was deranged?

Seemed like a lot of effort to go to.

What was his game? What did he want?

Stephen said, "You're working with the police, aye? On this missing schoolgirl case, the both of you?"

I nodded.

"What's this flat got to do with anything? My tenant?"

I said, "The girl in the pictures."

"That's her? The lass that's missing?"

I nodded again.

Stephen moved to sit down at the top of the steps. He took a few deep breaths.

I sat down beside him.

Earlier, I'd hoped Wickes was playing the good cop/bad cop routine. Well, here I was with the follow through.

Aye, I was there for Mr Stephen. To understand him. To empathise.

I was his friend.

My associate... he was just a headcase.

But I wanted Stephen to believe Wickes was harmless.

"He's emotionally involved," I said. "Knows the girl's mother."

"Emotionally involved? Is that a joke?"

I tried for a buddy-buddy smile. Did he relax? Looked that way. His shoulders quit hunching at any rate. "Not really," I said. "He needed inside the flat. To see for himself." Was I really making excuses for the man? "We're close to something, Mr Stephen. And I don't want to play down the fear you're feeling, but in the grand scheme of things –"

He turned and looked at me with eyes asking a hard question. "You're going to help the girl?"

I said, "Yes," and hoped that as he was looking into my eyes he couldn't see the doubt in them.

***

The Association of British Investigators has a code of ethics for all members. I sometimes wonder if that's why more people don't join.

One of the principle codes runs:

To verify the credentials of clients and that they have lawful and moral reasons to instruct an investigation.

In my rush to get on board, I'd taken Wickes on his word. Blinded by the thought that perhaps I would be doing some genuine good.

The nature of the job means that sometimes every investigator skirts the edges of ethical behaviour. The Data Protection Act means that grey areas crop up more frequently than they ever used to, stifling some operators who used to enjoy a more free reign in their practices.

But in my mind, I knew I had stretched one of the tenets of the Association to breaking point. Would it matter that my motivations were justified?

I met Wickes outside the building again. He was leaning against the car, casual and almost cheerful. "Why so glum?"

I could have lamped him.

Scared?

Aye, maybe a little.

I said, "This is a waste of time. We're out here chasing up dead ends and you know that every hour that passes –"

"I know the rule." He walked round the car, leaned on the hood. I had to spin to keep an eye on him.

"And what the fuck was all that about in there?"

He shrugged; what was I getting so mad about? "We needed to get inside."

"Why?"

"There had to be something. A clue or –"

"If we had time to waste," I said, "Maybe I'd say that was helpful. But you threatened a citizen, broke into a private dwelling and –"

Wickes waved a piece of paper in the air.

"Got us a fucking lead." He grinned, waggled his eyebrows. Would have been comical, maybe even endearing, if I couldn't still remember that look in his eyes when he'd pressed Stephen against the wall, threatened to squeeze the life out of the little man. "Found it in the kitchen. Pinned to the board. An address."

He laughed and started to cross the road to his own car. "The sister," he said. When he opened the car door, he paused, turned back and reached into his pockets. "Something else as well. You might be more interested in this one." He threw something in the air. It arced across to me, and I reached out and caught it in the palm of my hand. My fingers closed around the object, and when I opened them, I saw the cross that had been around Mary's neck on the video.

A vital lead, right enough.

Crucial evidence.

Which now had my fingerprints all over it.

***

People never tell you the whole truth.

No matter how much they trust you. No matter how much you trust them. When someone tells you a story, there's always something they miss out. Some little fact. Some detail.

They don't always mean to do it. It simply happens. Human nature.

We need the advantage. The upper hand. Something kept back. Our ace in the hole.

Wickes had found the slip of paper in the kitchen,

pocketed it fast before me or Stephen could notice. Pink paper, crumpled. Spidery handwriting.

An address.

A phone number.

A lead.

Maybe I was underestimating him. Had him all wrong.

One of the things I prided myself on as an investigator was my ability to read people.

Wickes had me all turned around. I couldn't even guess which way he'd jump next. So I had to wonder if that was really a bad thing, or if I was simply angry at myself for being unable to get into this guy's head.

For not living up to my own expectations.

Chapter 29

"Were they close? Deborah and her sister?"

We were in the Phoenix Bar, at the east end of the Perth Road. A small, comfortable pub with a regular bunch of drinkers and some of the hottest chilli on the North East Coast of Scotland. Check the menus, you'll see a burning ring of fire that's at once a warning of the heat and a reference to the old TV show, *Bonanza*.

We'd grabbed a corner booth, beneath the moose head that dominated one wall. The decoration in the Phoenix was best described as eclectic. Old adverts and framed images of the city as it once was dominated. A clock without hands was at one end of the bar.

Wickes was on pints of Timothy Taylor. I stuck with Coke, preferring to keep my head clear on a case.

The hard-drinking, hard-boiled detective only gets away with that shite in movies and between the pages of pulp paperbacks.

"I met the sister once," Wickes said.

"That's not what I asked."

There was an atmosphere between us. A distinct lack of trust that had been building since the incident at the flat.

I didn't trust his temper. Or his story.

It went both ways, of course. He no longer trusted me to stay on point. To back him up.

But he was talking. There was that at least.

"Deborah had some keepsakes she wanted to take with her. Stuff her sister had been looking after. Deborah couldn't face her sister. Not if she wanted to keep quiet about where she was going. So she sent me round."

Still not answering my question. But I figured I'd let him go with it. Maybe get my answers by accident.

Let someone talk long enough, they'll tell you things they never intended.

Wickes was a talker.

Wanted to hold everything back, but I got the feeling he couldn't resist giving up the truth in the end. His was the kind of personality that got bored easily.

Aye, check his impatience up at the flat.

The way he talked about Deborah and her problems. All the things most folks would keep quiet, he aired to a man who was at best a stranger.

Wickes licked his lips. Going dry. The effort of confession showing. His voice low.

I thought, as well: *dangerous*.

"The thing I remember is the way she looked at me. Even before I opened my mouth. Like I was detritus." He rolled the word around in his mouth. Savoured it. And then he looked right at me. "I was the reason Deborah was leaving the safety of her sister. Oh, the bitch knew that." I wondered if he even knew what he was saying. Could hear the words he chose. Understand how they sounded in my ears. "Sounds harsh, aye? Well you weren't there. Never met her. Cold fucking fish."

Less than a day into what I think he would have called our friendship, his mask was slipping.

The geniality. The transparency. The open-ness.

All an act.

But why?

A cover up? A carefully constructed persona? An echo of someone he used to be?

I wasn't sure. But he was beginning to let the façade slip in my company.

"We're both investigators," I said to Wickes. "Not bound by any fraternal code."

"One of the reasons I never wanted to join the ABI."

"But all the same, we have something in common. We look for the truth."

"Do we? My bread and butter came from heavy work. Muscle for hire. Or being a fucking errand boy."

"What do you mean?"

"Christ," he said, shaking his head before taking a deep drink from his pint. The head caught up his beard, and he wiped the back of his hand across his mouth to clear it. "You can be all noble and high-and-mighty dealing with the people who don't know, but we're barely fucking legal. We skirt the law. Dance around the edges of civilised society. Your precious ABI and the Security Industry Authority do their wee song about organising the profession, making sure we stick to a code of practice… but we're not really like that. None of us. How many members does your wee group have? Five hundred? Christ, and how many investigators are active in the country right now? On and off the books? We are not – should never be – accountable for what we do. We provide a service. A *private* service. One that should not be bound by the same rules that exist for the police or other state owned and run organisations."

Looking at him, I could see a fire in his eyes.

The fire of the man trying to convince himself more than anyone else.

Fuck trying to make a connection with him.

"You've been lying to me," I said. A weight lifted.

"About?"

"I don't know," I admitted. "Something. Holding out."

He nodded, seemed to consider this. Said, "Maybe I made a mistake. Coming to you for help."

"Maybe you did at that."

He took a deep swig from his pint, slammed the glass onto the wooden table. Never once took his gaze off me.

"We're going to the police," I said. "We're telling them everything."

"Fuck you," said Wickes.

I sat back in the chair. "This is how it works."

He laughed at that. Not the strange animal sound I'd come to expect from him, but a lower sound that rolled out from him and seemed to languish across the table.

I suppressed the urge to shiver.

***

"Susan Bright."

I hesitated when she answered. Not sure what I wanted to say.

Again, she said, "Susan Bright," with just enough impatience in her voice to goad me into

174

saying something.

"It's me."

"This isn't a good time for a social call."

"We need to talk."

"There's a girl missing, Steed. And unless –"

"This is about her. I think we might… I mean, this could help you."

The wind was blowing hard through the streets of the city. The cold of the past few weeks was getting worse, and heavier snow was expected, maybe even hoped for.

Slush was probably the best we'd get.

Susan said, "You know something?" her words were partially obscured as the line crackled.

I bowed my head to try and reduce the interference. "I know something."

She said, "Deborah Brown."

I said, "So you know. But maybe not everything."

Wickes was watching me from the shelter of the pub's doorway. He was leaning against the frame, his lips curled, his eyes focussed.

I tried to forget he was there.

On the other end of the line Susan relented, said, "Aye, right enough, maybe you've got a point. Maybe we need to talk. But it has to be good, Steed. It really does."

Chapter 30

The drive to FHQ, Bell Street, Wickes sat sullen. Fuming; refusing to look at me.

I remembered what had happened with Stephen earlier.

Anger issues?

Aye, took me long enough to figure that one out.

Which made me question everything he'd told me; helped me finally figure out why I'd been uncomfortable taking him on as a client in the first place.

I looked over at him.

He pretended not to notice.

At least he was coming with me. Had agreed to talk to Susan. I'd half expected him to blow up on me, maybe try and send me to the hospital for even daring to suggest he might need someone else's help.

I'd thought he was like me. That we connected somewhere with this need to sort out our own mistakes, to atone for things we'd done wrong.

More of his act.

I realised now we were nothing alike.

Or I had changed somewhere along the line and hadn't even realised until now.

***

Susan was waiting in the car park outside FHQ when I pulled in to the Market-Gait entrance.

Before he even got out of the car, Wickes twisted his neck to take a glance up at the blocky and imposing nineteen-sixties architecture of FHQ. Said his first words in over twenty minutes: "They all look the same."

Had to agree with him.

Susan waited at the base of the steps leading to the three sets of double doors that were kept locked on a close to permanent basis. No one really used the front entrance any more. A sign taped to the glass asked visitors to go to the rear entrance, where a bored member of Tayside's proud support staff sat behind safety glass and tried to figure out the time-wasters from the genuinely concerned citizens.

Susan held a plastic cup in her hand. The liquid steamed.

After we walked over Wickes said, "None for us?"

"This your new friend?" Susan asked, ignoring Wickes. "Is he going to tell me it was your idea to walk all over a sensitive investigation?"

Not even a smile.

Or a hello.

Officer Susan – pardon me, *Detective* Susan now – through and through.

I bulldozed past the cold front, sensing her concern was personal more than professional. Not wanting to get into that. Christ, we could keep the two apart, right? Said to Wickes, "This is Detective Constable Susan Bright."

He offered his hand. "He talks about you."

Susan didn't return the shake. Let him lower his

arm awkwardly.

Wickes said, "Temperature's down today."

Susan kept her eyes on me.

Said, "Deborah Brown... You told me this was about her. And Mary."

Wickes said, "Nothing to do with him. I was the one had the information. Made him keep it back."

Surprised me.

I'd expected sullen silence. Minimal co-operation. Maybe even some kind of outburst.

Susan finally looked at him. "Made him?"

Wickes smiled. Frosty. He was right about the temperature. "You wanted to talk about Deborah."

"It would help."

"How much do you know?"

Susan shook her head. "You don't ask the questions."

Wickes said, "Where's the DCI? Surely he should be here."

"I'm the one talking to you. This pans out, I'll have no hesitation taking it to the bosses."

Wickes looked at me. "You never said you had a thing going with a copper. Sly little bastard."

Susan said, "Eyes on the prize, moron. This isn't about some little soap opera in your head. This is about finding a girl who's gone missing. A girl who, statistically speaking, is probably already dead."

Wickes shook his head. "No. Not yet. She wouldn't... No, it's not in her."

"Then tell me what is. She's not exactly up for mother of the year."

"Christ, just let me... I can sort this out," he said.

"You're worse than this one," Susan said, gesturing at me. "What is it, a male thing? You're the only people who can sort out the world? All the bad

178

things would just go away if we gave you a chance to step up?" She shook her head, allowed herself a smile that had nothing to do with humour.

Wickes's jaw was clenched tight. A vein in the side of his forehead started to pump. "She's not dead. Deborah wouldn't kill the girl." That caught my attention. When he'd told me the story about the dog, that was precisely what he'd implied: Mary was in danger from Deborah.

Wickes kept going, "That's not what this is about." My imagination, or did I detect something like disappointment in his tone?

I didn't want to confront him with his contradiction, figured I'd wait and see where he was going.

"You're sure?" Susan asked.

"Oh, aye. I'm fucking sure, lass." I remembered how he'd been in the moments before he turned on Stephen.

Braced myself before stepping in, landing a restraining hand on the big man's arm. "She's not the enemy."

Wickes turned fast. Pushed me away. I stumbled, didn't go down.

"Of course she's the fucking enemy! Get real. Look at her, the lying bitch. You can see it in her eyes."

Susan held up her hands. "Maybe if we all calm down."

"Maybe if you go fuck yourself." Wickes turned his head to me and spat. A fat glob of spit smacked the ground next to my feet. "What, you think there's a chance she'll let you near her, so you believe every fucking thing she says? Fucking weak, man. I expected more of you."

I'd tried putting down his earlier outburst to frustration and anger at some kind of perceived impotence; the unconscious knowledge that there was nothing he could really do in this situation.

But I couldn't escape it: this man was driven by rage.

Susan said, "None of this is helping."

"Shut the fuck up," Wickes said, spinning back to face her. His body humming with the rage. "Little fucking cunt, all you want is control. Control over everything. Control you couldn't fucking handle if you got it." He stepped forward.

I saw what was happening. Couldn't quite believe it.

His fist raised. He roared; primal. The cry of a predator.

In the flat, when he went crazy and threatened Stephen, I'd been frozen to the spot. This time, I found myself tugging back on the giant's arm. Pulling him away from Susan. He shrugged me off, swatted his free hand at my face.

I barely felt anything; a rush of disorientation. My arms shot out to grab at something for support. Anything.

The world blurred. A noise battered through my skull; like putting a shell to my ear and instead of hearing the gentle lapping of waves, getting the scream of a storm.

I landed on my knees. Palms down, slamming into concrete. I tried to stay steady, shook my head to get the equilibrium back.

Something heavy landed on my back. My elbows gave way and I slammed straight down. My skull vibrated.

First thought:
concussion.

There were voices.

Footsteps.

On the back of my eyelids, I saw Susan at her father's party, lecturing me on something. Couldn't hear the words. Couldn't hear the voices. My face was on fire, pain searing up and along my cheek-bones.

Finally, I blacked out.

Call that a mercy.

Chapter 31

My leg was on fire. The calf muscles stretched to breaking point.

The surface beneath my back was hard and jagged. Could feel it even through my clothes. Figured it was concrete.

Okay, so what else did I know? I was outside. The air was too sharp for indoors. And the rush of traffic came from nearby.

Last thing I remembered was hitting the deck in the car park outside FHQ. Across the road from the old mills that had been converted to student accommodation.

I was still there?

Meant I hadn't been out long. Or they were afraid to move me.

Which begged the terrifying question of, *why*?

Not wanting to think about that, I tried to focus on anything else. Like the voice that sounded a long way away. Muffled. Indistinct. I had to concentrate to make out the words.

Realised it was Susan.

"If you can hear me, Steed, say something." She took my hand in hers. Her grip was soft, her skin warm. "Or squeeze my hand if you can't talk."

Her grip was insistent, concerned.

Comforting.

I thought: she can hold my hand forever.

I let out a breath. If I didn't say anything, she might not let go.

Drifted again.

Only thing I knew was the squeeze of her hand.

Only thing I wanted to know.

***

"Are you messing about this time? Or are you really awake?"

I opened my eyes. No effort, now.

No longer in the car park. On a sofa, my head supported by a balled up jacket. I could feel the zip line cold against my scalp, my hands flailing over the edge of the cushions.

My neck was killing me.

There was blood on face on my face; old wounds re-opened.

Keep going like this, you might eventually mistake me for a pro boxer. My left eye didn't quite open all the way. The world seemed soft around the edges. Nothing seemed to remain in focus for more than a second.

The skin around my eyes was puffed and tender. Hurt just to move my pupils. I wanted to reach up and touch; see how bad things were.

My conscious brain said: *bad idea*

So I was still thinking rationally. A good sign? Take hope where you can and all that shite.

I flexed my hands. My feet. Gave all my muscles a quick try; making sure I could move. Sure, they worked, but it was agony every time.

When I was satisfied, I turned my head – painfully slow – and saw Ernie Bright sitting in a bucket chair a couple of feet away. Watching me with this unreadable expression. He said, "Thought we were going to have to call a bloody ambulance." He checked his watch. "Just gone past eight."

Unreadable even if I knew that his very presence didn't exactly bode well.

I said, "Susan?" My voice came out harsh and broken, the effort of making the sound rasping the rear of my throat. I could imagine the muscles flaking.

"She's fine," Ernie said. "Although... she's got a shiner, right enough. The risk we all take, aye?" He was talking nonchalantly, but there was anger bubbling up. Susan was his daughter, after all. And even if he knew the job, knew that she knew the risks as well, none of that changed the way he felt about her.

I turned my head back so I was looking up at the ceiling.

The room was small. White walls. Strip lights. An office, maybe, decked out plain with a low coffee table, a cheap sofa and a few small chairs.

I figured interview room. Set for chats with witnesses and families. That kind of thing. More comfortable than any room in which you'd conduct an interview with a possible suspect.

I swung my legs. Made to sit up.

The world swung like a pendulum.

I toppled forward, grabbed the edges of the sofa to keep from going all the way.

Ernie didn't move a muscle. Aye, this man I'd called my mentor. Thought of as my friend.

Fuck him.

"DI Lindsay's been squawking in my ear," he said. "About the point my daughter insisted you'd be no hassle. Aye, goes to show how family's more trouble than it's worth. I didn't listen to the DI; he's an arsehole, right? Everyone knows it. A good detective, but a lousy people person. Maybe that's the way to be. Buggered if I know." Each sentence sounded disjointed. As though he didn't realise he was speaking any of them out loud, was simply trying to sort out his thoughts.

I said, "You're regretting letting me anywhere near the Furst case." Could have been a question, but I got the feeling he'd snap if it was.

He let out a little cough, as though clearing his throat. Smoothed out his trouser legs. Not preening. Just searching for a distraction. Maybe so he didn't have to listen to himself. "Do you get it yet?" he asked. "That my daughter's got a weak spot for you? Christ knows why, but there it is. And if you've got her ear, then I guess you've got mine too. Except... not any more."

Aye, message received: I'd fucked up.

So what else was new?

I leaned forward, tried to keep my back straight. My stomach was churning. Vomit backed up at the base of my throat.

I gulped in air, waited until my insides were settled and said, "You love her so much, you ever tell her about you and Burns?"

He nodded. He'd been waiting for me to bring that up. "Surprised you hadn't told her already." Did he sound surprised? Grateful?

185

Hard to be sure. Either I'd lost my touch, or he was putting on a fantastic bluff.

I leaned back. Grateful for the support of the sofa, but trying for a relaxed *like-I-give-a-toss* look. "Figured that was your call."

"Police work can be unpleasant," Ernie said. "In more ways than one when you start ascending the ranks. I never told you that one, eh? Didn't want to scare you off."

"Oh aye, I bet it's lonely at the top. Tell me; you're one of the reasons no one ever touched the bastard?"

He sucked in breath between gritted teeth. Looked like I'd pushed him onto the back foot. "I don't like your tone."

"I don't like that you're keeping secrets from your daughter."

He looked ready to launch from the chair. His eyes were wild.

I could have wept for the man I believed him to have been.

More, I could have wept for Susan.

When I left the force, I burned a lot of bridges. Some of them intentionally. Others, like Ernie, I just quit caring about.

Susan had tried to stop me from being an eejit, reached out to me, tried to keep me human. And when I pushed her away, she kept insisting until I finally let her in. I owed her my life. Literally and figuratively.

She found out about her dad... Christ only knew what it would do to her.

Ernie said, "Speaking of secrets, why don't you tell me about your friend? The bruiser with the beard?"

"Way Susan was talking, I though you lot knew

everything already."

"We didn't know about him."

"Maybe I should be talking to Susan."

"I'm the investigating officer, you jumped-up turd."

"You're a corrupt, ageing bastard."

We were silent, then. Both surprised by our own outbursts.

Tell me I had any lingering feelings of that old mentor relationship left behind.

He sat back. Quick, like I'd just slapped him one. Maybe I had at that.

***

When Ernie left the room, I swung my legs off the sofa, planted my feet on the floor and doubled forward; an approximation of the emergency-crash position. The one they call, *kiss-your-ass-goodbye*.

Someone once told me that the reason they have you lean forward is so that if there is a crash, then your head is jolted forward against the back of the seat in front and your neck is broken. Quick death. Better than the slow one if things go wrong.

Never bothered to find out if it was true. Like most urban legends, it remains unsubstantiated and half-heartedly denied by those who should be in the know. But it felt right. Enough air of morbidity to be based on fact.

Susan came into the room after maybe fifteen minutes. Her dad hadn't been joking about the shiner. She looked pale, and the black bruising around her seemed all the worse for her colouring. She even walked with a slight limp.

I said, "Bloody hell."

She shot for tough: "You looked in the mirror lately?"

"I try not to. Even on the best of days."

"Explains a lot."

What do you say to that?

Finally: "You have to tell me."

"About Wickes?"

She nodded. Patient. "Aye. About Wickes. And then later, you can tell me what's up between you and my dad."

"You know he was never happy about me leaving the force."

She forced a smile and raised a finger. A teacher ticking off a cheeky child. "Nuh-uh. No way, this is something else."

She could read me easily. Always the same.

Only one other person had been able do that.

I said, "What do you know about Deborah Brown?"

She gave me the basics. The surrogacy off the books. The complaints filed. The disappearance.

Tallying up with Wickes's story.

What had worried me from the start had been his emphasis. The facts he chose to linger on. The emotions he evoked when he spoke.

I told her what I could about Deborah Brown. She listened intently, waited until I was finished before saying, "And that prick Wickes says she's unstable?"

I nodded. "I believed him at first."

"And now?"

Did I have to answer?

"I've seen the video," I said. "At Deborah's flat. No denying it's Mary. I went to the school. Talked to the rector."

Susan nodded. She was interviewing me. This

was not about friendship. Or anything close to it. Oh, no, this was business. She took a deep breath, ran a hand through her hair. "You don't think she's behind the abduction?"

"I don't know if she means the girl harm."

"Aye, because you abduct the people you love."

"Right now," I said, "I doubt anything that Wickes told me is true. Whatever he says in interview, I wouldn't quite –"

Susan reached up to touch the swelling around her eye. Deliberate? Christ, I hoped not. "Bastard legged it."

"Yeah?"

"Fast on his feet for a big guy."

"I noticed."

"We're checking on him, now."

I nodded. "You won't find anything. "He's too clever for that."

"I wouldn't call assaulting a police officer clever."

"No," I said. Thinking maybe I'd call it desperate.

What was it I'd said before? Aye, love makes you do crazy things.

Maybe Wickes knew that better than most.

Chapter 32

I refused a trip to the hospital. Figured I'd sort my own head out.

I'd seen enough of Ninewells to last me a lifetime. Hospital was the last place I wanted to be.

***

I remember being in a hospital bed. A private room. Uniform outside the door like they thought I was going to get up and walk off.

My hand shattered.

Woozy with drugs and exhaustion.

DI George Lindsay came walking in. His simian slope enough to make me want to shout, "keep your paws offa me, you damn dirty ape." Guess I had enough sense left in me to keep my big mouth shut. Or else I was just too tired to care.

He scraped over a chair beside the bed.

"This isn't an interview," he said. "That comes later."

I nodded.

An hour or so earlier I'd been in a graveyard, with

my hand freshly broken and a gun pointed at the head of a London hard man who seemed the perfect scapegoat for all the pain and suffering I had witnessed.

I would have killed the bastard, too. If Susan hadn't shown up. Hadn't made me realise what the fuck I was doing, that I was ready to become exactly like the man before me.

"I'm here," Lindsay said, "To tell you that I know you're going to shite me off. I'm not an eejit, even if you keep believing that. No, pal, I'm a fucking copper. A good one, too. Heavy handed? Oh, aye. A cunt? Spot fuckin' on."

Hard to believe a man like Lindsay came here just to tell me that I'd been right all along.

"I'm here to tell you that you'll get away with it this time. Not because I like you. Not because you're innocent – nobody's innocent, you know that, aye? – but because you'll weasel your way out of it. Because that stupid wee lass with her head full of ideals seems to like you. Because you'll get fucking lucky, pal."

He leaned in close.

I could smell onions.

"Luck doesn't last forever. I know that. And somewhere in that thick skull of yours, I know that you know it, too. So if you get out of this, maybe you want to give it a rest. Because the minute you stick your size bloody twelves in, that's when things get fucked up. I've known that about you, pal, from the minute we met. You're a man with a conscience and a code and all that other bollocks, but you're also a man who drags his own disaster around with him like a wrecking ball. You want to help people. But you can't. Can't even help your fucking self."

Maybe he got to me, then.

I remember this shiver that ran through my body; a thousand ants scuttling just below my skin.

I'd blame it on the drugs, of course.

How could I ever admit that a man like Lindsay got to me like that?

And how could I ever admit that I thought he was right?

***

Back home from the station, I slugged aspirin, decided to hit the sack. Sleep it off. I'd had worse than this.

I drifted off, spent the night passed out.

Needed the rest. Clearly.

When I woke up, it was past eleven in the morning. Something was battering at the inside of my skull.

Something I'd forgotten.

I threw off the sheets, and got to my feet. Stumbled through to the kitchen, my legs unsteady. My muscles protested, but I ignored them.

This *thing* – this idea – refused to leave. It was like seeing something on the periphery of your vision, but every time you turn to catch it, it floats out of view again.

The kettle rumbled on the worktop.

I massaged my temples hard, as though I could somehow work loose this idea which seemed to be so desperately calling for my attention.

The kettle boiled. The switch clicked.

The idea slipped into focus.

The sister.

The paper Wickes had pocketed at the apartment.

I'd almost forgotten about it.

Deborah's sister.

The one Wickes had talked about like she hated him.

Why would Deborah have her address?

Why would Wickes pocket it?

I walked back through to the bedroom, forgetting about the kettle, and grabbed my jacket from where I'd slung it on the end of the bed. I dug inside the pockets. Pulled out the little cross on the chain.

Let it dangle between my fingers.

Chapter 33

This work, you need a good memory. Facts, figures, faces, names, attitudes; they all need to be kept straight in your head. You get nowhere if you start to forget things, fuzz up cases and people.

I'd never played the game like amateur hour. Call that a matter of pride.

Concussion counts as an excuse?

Maybe to some.

I was trying to recall what I'd seen on the paper. The address. Sitting in the spare bedroom, lit up by a desk lamp, writing down names and words on paper, concentrating on the memory of that wee pink square I'd seen in Wickes's grasp earlier.

It had been important.

Time ticked by. Hours. I struggled. My head was swimming. If I sat back, I'd drift off again.

Every time, that nagging insistence would pull me back out of sleep.

But it was slow going.

How hard had I gone down in the car park?

I should have been paying attention to Wickes.

Not allowed myself to be distracted by suspicions and conspiracies. Maybe then I wouldn't be locked up in a spare room trying to drag some half-remembered scrap out of information out of the useless lump of grey matter inside my skull.

But it wasn't just that. Sure, I'd refused to go to hospital, but I recognised the fuzzy feeling in my head, knew I wasn't at my best. My memory wasn't working properly: things seemed more confusing than they should have been. I couldn't separate out every fact I wanted to.

All I wanted was one piece of information.

Something that could help me connect the dots.

This was *important*. I wasn't about to be responsible for yet another fuck up. I was going to get all the evidence together, present it to Susan, let her deal with it.

That bastard Lindsay wasn't going to be right about me.

But I wasn't calling Susan until I had hard evidence.

Same old story.

The psychiatrist I'd seen after the crash – mandatory counselling, so the big boys on the force had called it – had unofficially diagnosed me like this:

"You have to be the hero. Save everyone. Doesn't matter if you know it's a bad idea. It's a compulsion. To satisfy your own ego."

I'd called shite.

Knowing he had my number down cold.

But who'd admit to that?

I closed my eyes, tried to see that paper.

Got nothing.

Threw the pen and paper across the room. Wanting to roar.

My head was bulging from the inside out. That pain even worse than ever, now.

My hand was buzzing.

The muscles in my left leg were screaming. As though stretched to breaking point.

I leaned back in the chair, locked my fingers behind my head and pulled my hands together. Tried to squeeze all the pressure out from inside my skull.

I closed my eyes.

The thing with this job, so much of it is logical procedure. Simple steps lead you to every solution. You need to remain methodical.

You can't remember an address, there's always some small thing you can do. Some tiny, intuitive practice that should come to you natural as breathing.

Remind me how hard I'd slammed the concrete?

Fuck my memory; Swiss-cheesed as the fall had made it. Let my fingers do the walking.

***

A name.

Kathryn Brown.

Came to me in a moment, as though something in my head just turned and clicked into place. That was all I needed. That first step, I could stumble the rest of the way.

What had Wickes called her? Aye, "the bitch". That and the way he reacted to Susan, I had to wonder how much love was really in his heart for Deborah.

One name is all you need. A name, enough information to guess at where they'd roam. Most people don't move so far. Aye, sure this is the age of mass transport, but the fact of the matter is that most folks stay where they're comfortable. Within a day's drive of the place they consider home.

Makes them easy to trace.

Especially if they're staying on the grid.

Information is everywhere. The modern world is a mass of facts and figures, most of it unsecured. People think they're being careful, they don't know the meaning of the word.

Without thinking, we give names and addresses to unsecured agencies. We willingly put ourselves on the electoral register. We give our whole lives out to the world in plain view of anyone who knows where to look.

A straight citizen like Kathryn Brown wouldn't be hard to trace. Made me wonder why the police hadn't done so already. Could be any number of reasons, of course. Most of them bureaucratic.

That was part of why I'd struck it out on my own. Any mistakes in my investigation would be my own and no one else's.

Of course, some days that was no comfort at all.

Chapter 34

"So where are you now?"

Susan knew exactly where I was. No question she could hear the rush of the engine on her end of the line. She was deliberately playing dumb; seeing whether I was still pulling those same old dance moves.

A little honesty doesn't hurt every once in a while. "I'm about ten minutes from her place."

She grunted. I could hear the disappointment.

Felt it a little myself.

What happened to passing this one off to the people best placed to deal with it?

I tried for light-hearted. "Figured telling the truth might stop you killing me."

"We'll see." Did I hear a barely disguised laugh behind that?

I tried to reason with her. Or at least convince myself I was doing the right thing. "If we go in like a raiding party and drop our size twelves all over her carpet, we're going to spook this woman. I think she knows where Deborah is – where Mary is – but I don't think she's going to want to talk to a whole platoon of fucking coppers about it. She's known the truth from the start; I don't think she wants to give her sister up."

"But she'll talk to you? She'll tell you everything?"

"I'm not a copper."

"That gives you some kind of privilege?"

"What I'm saying is… if you come alone, don't flash the badge, maybe between the two of us we'll be able to figure out what's going on. Find Mary. Bring her home."

There was silence on the other end of the line.

"Wickes was lying from the start. I think Deborah has Mary, but I think there's more going on here than we realise."

"You're angry that you fell for his sob story."

"Aye, you're right."

"You want to fix this yourself." She didn't even give me a chance to answer. "Look what happened last time."

I hit the brakes for red lights. Idled. Hands gripping the wheel. The leather slipped beneath my palms.

Susan said, "But I'll go with you on this. If nothing else, I want to be there to stop you. Before you make the same mistakes you did before."

"I'm a different man."

"Really?"

"You need someone to back you up," she said. "Watch out for you. I know you think things have changed, but you don't just come up for air from the kind of place you were in last year."

The lights changed. I hit the accelerator. "I'll see you there," I said, ignoring what she had just told me. Fighting a strange shiver that had started to build inside me. I reached out with my left hand and terminated the connection.

***

Here's what I knew about Kathryn Brown before I pulled up outside her house:

Homeowner. Decent credit rating. No outstanding debts. Kept her head down and stayed out of trouble.

She was unmarried. Held down a decent job with the forestry service that didn't involve going into the great outdoors terribly often. Had resided at the same address for the past five years.

I had her home phone. Address. Yearly salary.

Took two hours to pull all of that.

If you know where to look, you can find out things about people they'd never expect you to know.

***

Kathryn Brown lived out near Camperdown. A two storey Georgian house with a small front garden and driveway. Neat and minimal from outside. Nice place, bought during the housing boom. In the current climate, repossession had to be a worry.

In the current climate, everything was a worry.

The front door was painted dark blue. Recent job if I was any judge. Frosted glass at head height. I could see my splintered reflection looking back at me.

I rang the doorbell.

Lights were on. Someone was home.

The woman who answered was in her early to mid

forties. Her hair was swept up and her makeup was smooth and subtle. Some signs of age in her features, noticeably creasing around the eyes and mouth. But middle-age hadn't quite left behind the soft eyes and shy attractiveness of youth yet. See her in the right light, you'd be kind enough to guess at early thirties. She was dressed for the office in a sobering skirt-suit and silk blouse. Her expression was bemused and a little harried. Figured I'd caught her just in from work.

"Hello?"

I hesitated. Just a moment. She sensed it, too, took a step back and looked ready to close the door in my face.

I said, "It's about your sister. Deborah. And her daughter. We need to talk about that. We really do."

All things considered, she remained calm. Stepped back and let me walk inside. No protest.

Chapter 35

As I stepped inside, Kathryn Brown said, "I thought you might be the police. Except maybe for..." She gestured to her own face, meaning she'd noticed my new scars. And who wouldn't?

"The police?" Aye, check the innocent tone.

She led me through to the kitchen. The sliding French doors that led out to the rear of the property had been broken; glass shattered and spread out across the linoleum. "Happened before I came home. Five years I've been here, and no trouble." She nodded out across the back garden to the silhouettes of the high rises. "Sometimes wonder if the problems are worse in people's heads."

I said, "Comes to us all sooner or later."

She nodded. "You're sure you're not the police?"

I smiled. "Used to be."

She nodded. "You have the walk." She kept her back to me, started examining the shattered window, assessing the damage. A B&E, executed with no hint of subtlety.

I kept back. Looked around the kitchen. All the

utensils were packed away. All the work surfaces sparkled.

Funny thing was, I would have expected more chaos in the wake of a B&E.

When I looked back at Kathryn Brown, she offered me a sad little smile and said, "I think I scared them off when I came home."

"You saw someone here?"

She ignored the question: "When you mentioned Deborah, I was ready to shut the door in your face."

"You know where she is." Not a question. A statement of fact. She couldn't argue with me.

"Who are you again?"

I pulled out a card, laid it on the kitchen worktop. She looked at it, but not closely.

"Unusual job," she said.

"It pays the bills."

"Oh? Surprised we don't have more of you, then."

"Discretion," I said, "is the key."

She smiled, picked up the card and slipped it into the inside pocket of her suit jacket. She moved to the sink, grabbed a glass from the draining board and poured herself a water straight from the tap. Let it run for a few moments before placing the glass in the stream.

Splash back bounced off her hand.

"Tell me why you left the police."

I didn't say anything.

"I mean, what kind of man gives up on that? Goes on to become –"

I had to smile. "Aye, I know the reputation we have. Sleazy. Last resorts. Ray Winstone plays us on the telly as overweight, out of shape and morally dubious. Think the profession would keep going if we were really like that?"

She smiled.

The temperature in the kitchen was close to freezing with that hole in the rear door.

"Really," I said. "We need to talk about Deborah."

"I haven't heard from her in fifteen years."

"Then why did you let me in? I turn up, say I know you're hiding something, and you just let me waltz through your front door?"

"Couldn't have you outside," she said. "There's a frost lying." She led me into the living room. The room was lit by standing lamps from Ikea and the television was on *Sky One*. the volume turned low. A repeat of *Stargate*. She looked at the telly and then at me. Smiled uncomfortably and said, "I just like to have something on for the company. Why are you here and not the police?"

"The police never made the connection," I said.

"And you? How did you make it? What's your interest in any of this?"

"You mean am I just hunting glory?"

"It's a big story. You find the missing girl, it means a lot of coverage and a lot of business."

I nodded. "Remember the word *discreet*?" Business wouldn't pick up. An investigator's reputation with his clients often relies on their business not hitting the front pages.

She perched on the sofa across from me. Gestured for me to take a seat in the armchair opposite.

"I was looking into Mary's disappearance," I said. "Working with the police. Not in any official capacity. More as a... consultant."

She looked at me, one eyebrow raising of its own accord. Aye, what reason did she have to believe anything I said?

Trying not to sound uncomfortable, I said, "I got

204

involved because of a friend. A reporter working the story. He asked me to keep an eye on the situation."

She nodded. "Hardly noble."

I shrugged. "What is, these days? I was working the case, figured the connections with David Burns. And then I met a man who told me about your sister."

She stiffened. Knew who he was before I said anything.

Of course she did.

You don't forget a guy like Wickes.

"He came to me," I said, repeating myself a little. Trying to force the fact we had no connection. Would I trust anyone who said he knew that bastard? "He's looking for your sister. Get the feeling you know who I'm talking about? Calls himself Wickes."

She nodded. Still didn't say anything.

Who was to tell her I wasn't working with Wickes?

I tried not to sound too much like I was begging for her belief. "He gave me some story about how your sister kidnapped her daughter. I don't think it's entirely true."

"He's unstable," she said. "A head-case, you know?"

I almost said, "He says the same about her," but caught myself in time.

Did this mean she believed me, or that she was testing me?

She looked at me with a flat expression.

I nodded. Reached up and touched the new scars on my face. "I guessed that one."

"You got off lucky," Kathryn Brown said. "He's a killer."

I nodded. Sat forward in my seat. Said, "Tell me."

She hesitated.

"He's looking for your sister," I said. "If Wickes is as dangerous as I think he is, and half as smart, then he's going to find her. She can't keep running."

I paused for a moment, let that one sink in. "I guess you already know that. She can't do this alone. You can't do this alone. Let me help you. Let me help her."

"And Mary," she said. "More than any of us."

Chapter 36

Take three statements from three people and they'll all differ.

Sometimes in minor ways, but there'll always be a different emphasis, a different focus.

Sometimes all three will lie to aggrandise or diminish their own part in proceedings. What you do – as an investigator – is you take all these stories and pull them apart; find the kernel of truth in each one.

No one can lie convincingly without incorporating some element of truth into what they say.

Wickes hadn't lied about the surrogacy. The obsession, from a certain point of view, was also true. And the intimidation. That part, he had dead on.

The rest, according to Kathryn, was warmed-over shite.

"Deborah was looking for help. Someone to get Burns to cool off. The police were no help. Even when those bastards assaulted her. When they…" She broke off. What had happened the night those thugs broke into Deborah's room?

Wickes had been fuzzy on details.

Deborah's sister was avoiding them.

Maybe I already knew, but I hoped to Christ I was wrong.

"The police didn't do anything?"

"Didn't take her seriously. Kept giving her this shite about Burns being nothing more than a businessman."

Aye, try getting them to say that today.

Back then, it had been the end of the honeymoon for coppers and organised crime. No more backroom deals or attempts at negotiation. Zero tolerance.

Both sides coming to terms with the end of an era.

I said, "You remember the name of the officer she talked to?"

Kathryn shook her head. "It was a long time ago."

What was the bet... Bright?

Christ, and why not? He couldn't go down any further in my estimation, right?

"If you people had just done your job, maybe we wouldn't be here, now."

You people.

I wasn't a copper any more. But I still carried their sins.

The job of an investigator is often nebulous; our precise areas of interest fuzzy and undetermined. More often we can say with certainty what we can't do rather than what we can.

The *Britain's second police force* slogan sometimes feels like just that. An empty collection of words designed to inspire faith without actually saying anything of value.

People come to us to track down missing persons, gain evidence on other's activities and sometimes to hire muscle.

The intimidation game.

A no-no for anyone on the ABI register.

Wickes had done that kind of work. In the old days, most people in the profession wouldn't have thought twice about it.

These days, the lines are defined more clearly.

"All she wanted was someone who could get these people to leave her alone."

The way Wickes told it, she came to him looking for a saviour. That had been where his story made the connection between us: who could refuse that kind of request?

"He told her it would never happen. What she needed to do was run."

Kathryn nodded. "When she came and told me that it was better to run away than to fight, it sounded sensible. Given... the situation. And the authorities' lack of interest."

"But he persuaded her to run away with him. He offered her the protection she needed. Or thought she did."

"That's what I didn't like. This man – this man she barely knew, barely trusted – offering her a way out."

Talk about your deals with the devil.

There were conditions to the arrangement. A whole book of them. The one that worried Kathryn the most: Deborah was allowed no contact with her old life. She would have to leave everything behind.

Including her sister.

"And she just went along with that. Always Deb's problem, you know? She was... suggestible. Never knew if that was to do with... you know..."

Her depression. Her illness. Kathryn didn't need

to say anything out loud. I could sense it, what she meant. What she didn't want to say.

Wickes hadn't been lying to me about some things, at least.

She must have seen my look, said, "Aye, you know, then?"

"Way he told it, she was aggressive and unpredictable."

Kathryn's eyes were glassy. Puffed up; those bags showing.

It was killing her just to talk about any of this.

But she had to.

And I had to listen.

Chapter 37

I went to the kitchen, found the kettle and the tea.

Set the kettle boiling, checked outside the door to see if Kathryn was anywhere to be seen. Figured she wasn't much up for going anywhere.

I kept my distance from the broken glass, figuring when they finally got round to it, the first officers on the scene weren't going to appreciate someone trampling the scene. I looked at the French doors; the gaping hole to the night outside. Wouldn't feel safe myself with that kind of damage overnight. Had she called for help? When I came to the door, she thought I was the police, which made me ask: where were they?

Response times were an issue these days; every couple of months, the local papers made a noise about how the police weren't responding appropriately. Like they understood the kind of pressures the lads were under, especially the boys on the beat.

I pulled out my mobile, dialled Susan's number.

"I'm nearly there."

"Leave the badge outside," I said. "Don't tell her

you're a cop."

I could sense the anger on the other end. "I'm not lying to anyone."

"I'm not asking you to lie. Just to… omit certain facts. Look, she's jumpy, okay? And she doesn't trust the police. Not about this situation."

"She's got something to hide?"

"Doesn't everyone." I checked back the corridor again. I was talking low, a hoarse kind of whisper.

Susan went quiet on the other end of the line. I wondered if maybe she'd just hung up. Then: "I'll go with it," she said. "But if this is another wild goose chase, I'm arresting you for obstruction of –"

"Fine," I said, and hung up.

The snap of the phone echoed too loudly and afterwards, the house seemed uncomfortably silent even though the kettle was reaching a boil.

I made the tea fast, went back to the living room. Told Kathryn that an associate of mine was coming round.

"You want to know where Deborah is?"

"Yes," I said.

"She didn't abduct the girl."

I didn't know what to say. Mary was still under sixteen years of age, had disappeared from her home without her mother's knowledge. What else would you call it?

But I didn't disagree.

Like I'd said to Susan; no lies. Just omissions.

***

Kathryn Brown didn't like Wickes much before she met him.

When he came to pick up Deborah's things, she

212

liked him even less.

"You've seen him, the way he carries himself. He's a big man. Imposing." From the minute he walked in the door, she said, he treated her like shite. Practically pushing her out the way as he made straight for Deborah's belongings.

Kathryn put it succinctly: "This was the man she said she was falling for."

Aye, they'd had the heart to heart. Deborah had come to her sister for advice about Wickes's plan. Uncertain, but undecided. Talking as though Wickes was some kind of rough-edged saint.

Nothing close to the man who barged past Kathryn, who called her an uncaring and manipulative bitch.

"The thing that struck me... not his size. But... I remember looking at his eyes, and... I don't know. You've seen these wildlife documentaries? The small animals take one look at the predator bearing down on them and it's like they've been hypnotised? Like that. I was scared. I'm not afraid to admit it, either."

Looking into someone's eyes, seeing evil there, it's the kind of description I'd dismiss as overactive imagination. If I didn't know Wickes. Hadn't seen his true self shifting uneasily beneath the mask he wore.

"He came to the door angry, like I'd already refused him entry before he knocked. Didn't say hello. Barged past me. The kind of strength in it, I don't think he cared if he hurt me or not." Kathryn massaged her hands as she talked. Maybe feeling guilt at not having done anything for her sister fifteen years ago.

I wanted to ask her why she didn't do or say anything. Why she didn't act on her instincts.

It's easy to judge.

I've had to teach myself to step back. Understand that people are their own judges in the end. Consciously or unconsciously we all punish ourselves.

"He went straight to her room. Like he'd been there already. Although I'd never met him before. Never seen him in the house."

"Did you talk to him?"

"I tried."

"And?"

The real hesitation. Right there. The massaging became intense and she started looking around the room.

"And?"

She couldn't escape. Maybe realised it would only compound her first mistake. She drew a long breath, raised her head. "I talked to him. Tried to." She shifted on the sofa, played with her blouse, pulled it up to reveal her lower abdomen. The left hand side.

An ugly blotch on pale skin. Blackened and cracked and wrinkled; the kind of wound that doesn't heal quickly. Doesn't allow you to forget.

She let the silk drop back to cover it, and fell back onto the sofa. Her eyes damp and her face pale with exertion.

What had it taken to show me that?

I said, "He did that." Wanted it to be a question. But it wasn't. I knew the answer. Made my stomach churn.

She nodded. "I asked too much," she said. "Insisted. All I wanted to know was whether he'd take care of my sister, if he'd really look out for her. You know, I just didn't like what was happening. Needed to hear from someone other than Deborah that –" She crumpled in on herself. Doubling up. Her body shuddered.

Across the other side of the coffee table, I couldn't offer any comfort.

Didn't know if there was any I had to give.

"I'd been ironing," she said. "When he came round. Ironing. The kind of thing… it's a chore, aye? Boring. Mundane. Not dangerous."

I closed my eyes. All I could see was that scar. The puckered skin. The angry outline.

The kind of scar that stays with you.

"I asked him about my sister. Over and over. He didn't answer. I grabbed his arm. He turned round. I slapped him." She spoke with slow deliberation. There would be no faltering. She'd lived with this for years. Now she could tell someone. Someone who would listen.

She talked with the inevitability and rising momentum of an avalanche. "That was when he grabbed me. I remember thinking he was going to break my arm. Just twist and… *snap!* That's what I was waiting for. Feeling sick at the thought of it, aye? But it never came. The pain, not like that."

Sitting in the calm of her house, I tried not to think about it. But couldn't help imagining Kathryn fourteen years younger being grabbed into the spare room where she'd been ironing, listening to the radio. *Being thrown to the floor.*

The big bastard looming over her.

First time I saw Wickes, I'd had this mental impression of him as The Big Friendly Giant and Brian Blessed's unholy love child.

The truth was nothing so reassuring.

Over the past day and a half I'd realised that he was nothing more than a force of sheer hatred.

215

Nothing discernible about it; just an absolute distaste for the world about him. A contempt for all the people.

But I'd only scratched the surface of his insanity.

Kathryn Brown had seen his true face.

Buried that memory deep for all these years.

What was it doing to her, reliving it in front of a complete stranger?

I wanted to reach out, tell her she could let it go. That she didn't have to do this.

More, I wanted to break something. Burn down the house where this had happened, purify the past in fire.

I wasn't just angry at Wickes.

But at myself for making Kathryn Brown relive that moment.

Not for her own sake.

But for mine.

So that I could know the truth.

Aye, tell me again, between me and Wickes, who really caused the most pain?

Chapter 38

Susan came to the door. When I answered, she reached out instinctively, touching my arm.

I could have collapsed. Let her catch me.

Tired.

So tired.

"It's fucked," I said. "All of this. Just... fucked up."

***

I introduced Susan as my "associate".

Kathryn hardly seemed to notice. She was still shaking.

Just before Susan had arrived at the door, Kathryn had said to me, "I should have done something else. I should have told someone. Gone to the police."

What do you say to that?

In the living room, I filled Susan in on the details. Kept them brief. To the point. No point re-opening wounds.

Kathryn remained silent.

Despite my brevity, I could see the steel set in Susan's face. She heard the story in the gaps I left.

When I was done, Susan took the lead talking to Kathryn. Maybe not flashing her badge, but I'd have taken her for a copper. Maybe Kathryn didn't care. Or believed that Susan was off the Job like me.

The two important questions:

Where was Deborah?

Where was Mary?

Her abrupt approach seemed to surprise Kathryn; a glass of cold water in the face.

I could hardly watch.

But the questions had to be asked. One way or another, time was running out. Even if Mary was in no danger from Deborah, there had to be a reason they had disappeared.

And I knew what it was, now.

I understood Wickes. What he really wanted.

What he really was.

***

The doorbell.

Kathryn went to answer.

In the living room we heard two officers at the front door.

Susan looked at me. Whispered, "I know those voices. If they come in here and start calling me *detective*..."

"We lose all the trust."

"And we lose our line to Mary." She took a breath, looked ready to lamp me one. "You know this is your fault?"

"Isn't everything?"

Susan stood up. "Lucky I need the toilet." She

218

could have smiled. Would have made me feel better, at least. But she didn't. The message loud and clear.

I kept still.

The two officers responding to Kathryn's call about the broken window were young. Probably fresh out of training college. The lad with the bad skin looked me up and down and said, "You're the investigator, then?" while his partner – a petite woman with an angular face and hard eyes – looked around the room as though expecting to discover some vital clue hidden in the corners.

I stood up, offered my hand. "McNee," I said. "Used to be on the force myself."

They both looked at my outstretched hand.

The girl said, "Heard of you." Flat. Emotionless.

I tried for an ice-breaking smile. "All good, I hope?"

"I worked a case with DI Lindsay a while back. What do you think?"

I dropped the outstretched hand. No takers.

What could I say? Working with Lindsay explained the eyes at least. And the suspicion. Christ, listen to what he had to say about me, you'd probably believe my real name was Beelzebub.

The lad said, "There's two of you here?"

"My associate had to go to the bathroom."

"And your... associate's... name?"

Good question. I tried not to look like I was fumbling. "Elaine," I said, and winced when I finished: "Elaine Barrow."

The lad nodded. The name meant nothing to him, but at least it was a name.

One that caught in my throat.

I looked at Kathryn Brown.

She didn't react.

Maybe we'd gotten through to her. Maybe she understood.

Or maybe she just wasn't listening.

I said to the lad, "Why the twenty questions? You're here about the window? The break in."

The girl nodded. Turned to me and said, "All the same, from what I've heard about you –"

"DI Lindsay and I have a history. Not a good one. I wouldn't listen to much he says about me. And I'd expect he'd say the same about me."

The lad said, "Maybe he's right. Maybe we should just –"

The girl cut him off: "Aye, fair enough. Although I think this is private, Mr McNee. Unless you have knowledge of the felony? Can I ask what you were doing between the hours of six-thirty and seven-thirty this evening?"

Check the impersonal, professional tone.

Sending me a message? No doubt.

I said, "I have business with Ms Brown. And even your friend, the DI, will tell you that a B&E isn't really my style."

Kathryn stepped in, said to the officers, "Maybe we could talk in the kitchen?"

As they left, the female officer turned to me and said, "I hope your associate's okay. She seems to be taking an awful long time in there."

I resisted making any smart-arse reply.

But only just.

***

The coppers' interview with Kathryn Brown was brief and perfunctory. Susan managed to stay out of their way until they left the building. They weren't interested in her, anyway. I think they were both disappointed to have little more than a bog-standard B&E on their hands; little in the way of witnesses and evidence. The girl in particular seemed especially upset that she couldn't pin anything on me.

Lindsay had trained her well. No doubt there.

They said it would take a while for SOCO to arrive, but that they doubted they would find anything useful. Until then, no one was to go in the kitchen. They recommended a 24 hour glass repair service who could block up the hole until a proper job could be done.

Of course, I wasn't listening in on the discussion. Not at all.

When the door closed, I was standing behind Kathryn Brown in the hall. Asked her, "Everything okay?"

"Nothing was taken. Looks like a random act of vandalism. You know how it is, sometimes. They reckon maybe I disturbed whoever it was when I got home and they went out the way they got in." She shrugged. "I've got a friend coming over with some polythene and duct tape. I'll have a *Blue Peter* house for a couple of days."

I nodded, turned to head back to the living room.

She said, "Tell me why you lied about your friend's name."

I stopped where I was. Susan came down the stairs, walked past me, looked Kathryn straight on and said, "I'm a police officer. A detective actually. CID."

"They'd recognise you, give the game away."

Susan nodded.

Kathryn said, "And then the trust is broken. But either way… Bright. The name's familiar for some reason." She walked past Susan and into the kitchen. We followed, neither of saying a word. Difficult to gauge her reaction.

In the kitchen, she stared at the shattered glass, kept her back to us.

Susan said, "We need to know where your sister is. We want to help is all."

Kathryn said, "I know the name. The DS, the one I talked to about Deborah. The one who told me not to worry, that I was being stupid. Jesus, ten years ago. More. I should know that when I look in a mirror, but when you stop and think about it… It's such a long time." She turned round to look at us. "His name was Bright, too. The DS."

I couldn't help but look at Susan.

She didn't react. Just nodded, and said, "It's in the past now, right? All of that. I can't apologise for mistakes made by other people. For oversights. Misunderstandings. All of that. I can only do my best to help you here and now."

Kathryn wrapped her arms around her middle and shuddered. Looked at us for a moment before she said anything.

Chapter 39

We took my car.

Drove north of the city, through Birkhill and out into the countryside. Passed the Templeton woods; gathered trees bowing together in a way that appeared unnatural, their dark spaces hiding secrets that would not be given up easily.

Maybe Susan was affected worse than me. Three months earlier she'd been involved in a murder case, the body found out in the woods in a shallow grave. An eighteen year old girl killed by a sad and desperate man who had been rebuffed one time too many. A man struck by his own actions who couldn't even bring himself to finish burying the girl's corpse.

"Do you ever long for the masterminds?" she said as we drove into the night.

"The masterminds?"

"The Hannibal Lecters. The Blofelds. The Jokers. The bogey-men from comics and films and books. The monsters we can never really identify with. The ones we'll never really know."

"The ones who make us feel safe?"

She nodded. "Because they're not real. Because if we ever saw them, we'd know they were the bad guys. I wish for that, sometimes. Something I could point at and say: that is evil."

I'd been a copper long enough to have seen the true face of evil. Not malevolent insanity, but mundane and petty jealousies and inadequacies. People drawn to commit unspeakable acts for reasons they could never explain or understand. You weren't careful, you could get dragged down by that. Pulled into a mire of disgust at what the human race was capable of.

Was I lucky to get out when I did?

Sometimes the world isn't the way you see it at all.

"She mentioned my father."

Caught me by surprise. I took in a sharp breath, composed myself and said, "I suppose he took the case when –"

"He palmed her off. That's not like him. I mean, she's talking about threats being made against another person by a known criminal element. He couldn't simply ignore it."

I hesitated. "He'll have had his reasons."

"Steed, you wouldn't be holding out on me?"

I didn't reply fast enough.

"Pull over."

"We don't have the time –"

"I thought we were friends."

I didn't want to tell her. Not now.

Later, maybe.

Or perhaps I could hold onto it forever.

She said, "Pull over and let me out. Or tell me what you know about my dad."

I couldn't look at her. Said, "It's all in the past. I

mean, he must have told you about the work he used to do in the bad old days. When the force was cutting deals with men like Burns."

"Not my dad."

"He was working under orders. I mean, the plan at the time –"

"Do you know what the first thing he taught me about being a police officer was, Steed? He taught me that no matter what you do, do not give men like Burns a break. You do not give them a chance to even pretend that they are in the right, that they have some kind of moral high ground that allows them to do the things that they do. Because if you do that, they've won. He'd fight against that kind of strategy. Wouldn't allow himself to get involved."

I almost laughed. Was thinking about Ernie standing in the back yard at Burns's house, holding his drink in his hand. Making me apologise for doing what every right thinking bastard wants to do to men like Burns.

I'd known at the time that it would kill Susan to know the truth. I'd hoped that the conversation would never come between us. That if she had to find out, then it wouldn't be from me.

I should have hidden this from her.

Denied everything.

But she could see right through me.

Or else I wanted her to.

"You should talk to him," I said. "But right now –"

"You're right," she said. "Right now, we need to think about the girl. About Mary."

We kept driving in silence. After a few miles, I turned to look at Susan. The moonlight caught her; surrounded her features with a soft light.

The set of her face made me think of Elaine.

Gave me that strangely sick feeling in my stomach again.

We were friends, Susan and me.

Could never be anything more.

We'd made that mistake once. I wasn't willing to try again, risk losing her friendship forever.

She turned and looked at me, her brow creased in what might have been a question. I turned my attention back to the road. Focussed on the broken white lines, the curve of the tarmac.

Neither of us said anything.

The lines started to blur.

Chapter 40

"There are some places where you simply feel safe."

That had been Kathryn Brown's response when we asked her where her sister was.

My first thought was the she was answering her own question, not even listening to what we asked. Sometimes, during our talk, she would become distracted, drift off into a place where I don't think either myself or Susan could follow her.

"We were close when we were girls," she said. "When we were eight or nine it seemed as though we would always do everything together. We were sisters. Inseparable."

A sadness washed over me as she spoke.

***

Elaine's family had always been close. Mother, father, sister; all of them inseparable in a way that had always made me jealous. Even after her death, they rallied around each other in a way that I felt I could never really be a part of.

I was an only child whose parents had died too young. Who had allowed himself to play the role that other people expected of him: distanced.

Not unfriendly, but never allowing anyone to get that close.

My all too brief sessions with the counsellor following the accident that killed Elaine touched on my anger, withdrawal and need for revenge.

And my childhood, of course.

Counsellors, psychologists, psychiatrists all have this strange fixation on what they call *formative experiences*.

My sessions were marked by resistance, anger and impatience. Didn't stop the bastard trying, right enough.

"You seem resentful."

He had no right to make judgements on me. His own ground rules were:

No judgement. No blame.

I guessed they were the kind of rules that only apply to everyone else.

Later, I'd try and apply the same rules to my investigative work. Ensure I was unbiased, uncompromised.

Of course, I was every bit as hypocritical as the doctor. Whenever those rules become inconvenient, it's easy to just throw them away.

"Resentful?"

Every session, I was one wrong word away from walking out the door. Forcing myself to stay because I thought I wanted back on the Job, back on the force. When I made the decision to leave the police, I'd give up on the sessions, too.

The word *mandatory* holds a great deal of power.

"Were you resentful of her family?"

228

We'd been talking about Elaine. Why I hadn't talked to her family since the accident.

He pressed the issue. The way he always did. "They're very close-knit. Would sacrifice anything for each other if they could." He paused, watching my reaction. I was careful not to give him anything. Looking back, though, my emotions were likely lit up like a fucking flare. "Your words. Not mine."

"No."

"So tell me about your family."

"Nothing to do with this."

"I know your parents died young."

"Define young."

He was holding back his outburst. No judgement? He couldn't help making them, the arrogant bastard. "Were you close?"

"They were my parents."

"Doesn't tell me much."

"You mean, were we like Elaine's family?"

He didn't give me an answer.

Two could play at that game, right enough. I still believed he had no business asking about my life, my inner thoughts.

What could he tell me that I couldn't tell myself?

Aye, maybe these days I have a few better answers to that question.

"You won't tell me?"

I shrugged. "Nothing to do with why we're here."

When Kathryn Brown talked about her family, it made me think about the Barrows. Close knit. Taking the kids on vacations even when they were old enough to move out on their own. The whole clan sharing a house in the middle of the French countryside every year, like nothing had changed between them. Even though they had their own lives, they could still go home.

The abiding rule of my life had always been:

You can never go home again.

I had nowhere from my past I wanted to revisit. Nowhere where I felt safe, where I would want to return when I wanted to hide. How could I hope to understand a woman like Deborah Brown?

It was no wonder that I had believed Wickes when he talked about Deborah's obsession. To anyone else, it would have seemed natural; an extension of her close-knit upbringing; a need for family that anyone else could empathise with.

I hadn't seen that. Hadn't considered it.

Wickes had talked about how we were the same. Burns had said similar things. And I was starting to wonder whether I really had more in common with these thugs and monsters than with anyone close to normal.

Chapter 41

The sun had set by the time we pulled off the main roads. I drove slow on what were little more than dirt tracks, focussed on what was ahead. The head-lights didn't seem to slice through the darkness so well.

The fog was falling along with the temperature. We hit pockets of white that reflected the full beam of the headlights back on us.

The car was forced down to a crawl.

I hit the interior light so that Susan could read the directions.

She kept looking out the windows, squinting slightly, "I hate the country."

"Really?"

She gave a little laugh, killed it quick. "I'm a city girl at heart. Streetlights, you know? Marvellous invention."

I still couldn't quite get over it; "*City* girl?"

"Dundee's a city."

"Hardly New York or LA. Not even Edinburgh."

"The city with the small-town heart. Isn't that one

of the slogans the council tried out a few years ago?"

"Some shite like that," I agreed. Since the late nineties, Dundee had been constantly trying to re-invent its public image. The problem was that until you spent any time in the city, old prejudices and half-truths stuck in your mind, coloured your view of the place.

What you saw from the outside was faded old buildings and empty factories, a downtrodden and desperate population trapped by the industries of the past that had left the city behind decades earlier.

It was a phenomenon, how only when you lived in the place did you discover another side. As though Dundee was desperate to keep itself hidden from outsiders. Seeing the true face of the city was something reserved for those who were prepared to take the time to understand it.

"The point is," Susan said, still craning her neck to look out for any landmarks and turnoffs, "that I like streets. And buildings. And signposts. Out here, everything looks the same. There's nothing to tell you where you are. One field is pretty much the same as the next."

We hit a curve in the road. The headlights spun, caught a sheep who was standing by a barbed wire fence looking out at us with curiosity, maybe having been awoken by our approach. Reflecting back the glare of the bulbs, her eyes took on a supernatural-looking sheen. I felt a shiver.

What was the old saying?

Aye, like someone had walked over my grave.

"Next turn off," said Susan.

"You're sure?"

"On the right."

She might have injected just a little authority into her voice.

It would have helped.

***

The building, as I had pictured it in my head, was a bright and sunny place. The front garden was well maintained – maybe with a few vegetable plots the girls would have tended when they were young – and there was an air of life and beauty to the structure that emanated from the brickwork itself.

Maybe I was just glomming onto Kathryn's childhood memories.

It had been years since anyone had come to the wee bothy out in the middle of nowhere. Kathryn told us how she had come up once since inheriting the building to check on its structural integrity. When she could find the time, she said, she was considering tarting the place up, selling it on.

"Sometimes the past needs to stay in the past."

Sing it, sister.

We rolled in front of the old cottage with its rough stone walls, single-glazed windows that glared balefully out at the night. The rickety front porch looked ready to blow over at the slightest hint of wind.

A rusty old axe was buried in an oak stump by the front door. I got the feeling no one had touched it for years.

Christ, happy childhood memories?

I'd have guessed nightmares, looking at the place.

But isn't that what happens as the years pass? Entropy and decay. Nothing remains the same. No memory is sacred.

The front garden was surrounded by a low pile of

rubble that might have once been called a wall. Weeds and long grass had become unkempt and unwelcoming.

As we pulled up, a dull light in one of the front windows suddenly extinguished itself. As though the house was trying to hide in the dark.

A beat up looking Ford sat beside the west wall.

I killed the engine and we sat there for a while.

Susan said, "She must have heard us."

I nodded in agreement.

"We need to do this now. Take control of the situation."

I nodded again.

Thinking about DI Lindsay sitting at my bedside, telling me how I was a human hurricane; a natural disaster of the worst possible kind.

What's the old song?

King Midas in Reverse.

I looked at Susan.

She hadn't wanted to be here. This wasn't how she would have done things. She'd been pulled into this by my own greed and my own need to do things that worked out best for me.

I couldn't help but wonder if the silence in the car was merely the calm before the storm.

I opened the door, swung my legs out of the car. Too late now for second thoughts.

Susan walked with me to the front door. Checked her mobile as we walked. "Another thing about the country," she said. "The great bloody outdoors." She shook her head. "No signal."

I nodded. We were isolated.

Susan said, "Have you even thought this through?"

How do you answer that?

A smart quip?

Or pure silence.

The last defence of the man with no defences left.

I stopped at the front door; a barrier I did not want to cross.

Was it too late?

Could I turn back now, forget about all of this?

Some things had changed over the last year. I like to think I was a different person than I had been.

But in the end, maybe not that different.

Chapter 42

Deborah Brown was five-two, with close cropped hair that had once been blonde and now edged to white. Her eyes were sharp, ten years younger than her features suggested and punctuated by crows feet and skin that had wrinkled more than it should have on a woman her age.

You could see the years of worry scored into her face.

She looked at me with her head tilted up and back. Ready to run. And why not? She had no reason to trust me.

"My sister called. Said you were coming."

Susan stepped out and in front, impatient with my silence. Said, "We need to see Mary. To know that –"

"She's all right?" Deborah gave a little laugh and dropped her head. She stepped back and gestured broadly for us to enter. "She's more than all right. She's with her mother. She's safe." She stood her ground, arms folded. "Just walk away from this. Tell everyone you couldn't find her. Make up whatever story you want."

I said, "You're protecting her from him, aren't you? Because you know what he'll do to her. What he does to everything you ever loved."

Her stance softened. Her head dropped.

I said, "I've seen him for what he is. The anger. The hate. All those other things you wish you'd seen right from the start. I can't imagine what it took for you to leave him. But you can't do this alone."

She laughed at that. "We're always alone," she said.

***

The croft was small. Four rooms off a main corridor with a rear door leading to an unkempt garden out back. The floors were uncarpeted and the walls roughly painted with whitewash that had cracked in places down the years.

I expected the smell of damp. Was surprised by how well the building was holding up, despite the shabby décor.

The living room – where we'd seen the dull light from outside – was large enough, decorated sparsely. The TV was on, tuned in through Bunny Ears to a fuzzy Channel 5. A girl was sitting in an old, sagging armchair and watching the picture intensely as though she could cut through the snow with sheer determination. Next to her sat an abandoned laptop and IPod with headphones.

Mary Furst.

She was taller than I expected, her legs longer, stretched out onto a ragged footstool. She was dressed in tracksuit bottoms and a white t-shirt, had her hair tied back in a loose pony tail. Loose strands fell across her heart-shaped face. She looked up as we came in, and I noticed the way her body stiffened.

Her legs recoiled off the footstool. Ready to bolt.

She only relaxed when Deborah came in.

Susan took the lead once again, stepping forward, introducing herself. Asking if the girl was all right.

Mary looked to Deborah as though for permission. I watched the older woman nod.

Saw something I hadn't recognised when Jennifer Furst had talked about the girl; a deep and unconditional love that could break your heart.

I reached into my pocket. Took out the cross I had found at Deborah's apartment. Walked to the girl, held it out so that the cross dangled between my fingers.

Mary looked at it. Her face screwed up, as though she was thinking hard.

I thought I saw a hint of tears in her eyes. But she blinked them away. Reached out, grabbed the cross and threw it away. It hit the far wall and fell to the floor.

There was silence as though no one knew what to say.

Finally, I turned to Deborah, "Maybe we can talk?"

She stepped back out into the hall. I took that for a yes.

Before I stepped out, I felt a hand on my arm. Turned and saw Susan, her face set hard, her eyes asking me something.

But I didn't know what.

***

We talked in the room across the hall. Guessed it was the bedroom. A couple of mattresses thrown down on the floor. Sleeping bags. A space heater running in the corner.

I looked around, said, "Frontier living." A joke to break the ice.

With that cold front on its way, we needed all the heat we could get.

Deborah didn't say much. Leaned against a wall and looked at me with those sharp eyes and an expression that made think of an eagle eyeing up its prey.

I said, "How much of his story was true?" Meaning Wickes. Getting straight to it. How much longer could I dance around the important things in life?

She laughed at my question. Frustrated rather than amused. The noise bounced off the walls and when it finally snapped off, it left the room feeling even more quiet than before.

The space heater hummed.

"He's a wanker," she said. "Insane. A killer. A sadist. A twisted… a twisted fuck." Her refined accent formed the harsh words awkwardly. But they came from somewhere deep inside; an immediate gut reaction to the mere thought of the big, hairy bastard.

I thought, *tell me something I don't know.*

***

Later, I'd talk to other people who had been involved. Check the records. Get the full story. Understand everything that happened nearly fifteen years earlier that led to the bloodbath of that cold winter night.

An investigator's work makes sense of people's fractured lives. Weaving everyone's individual truths and experiences together in ways that might eventually make some kind of sense.

Sounds grand, doesn't it?

A calling.

Wish I could always see it that way.

***

Her childhood may have been idyllic, but as she grew up, Deborah Brown started to hate herself. Her family. Everything around her.

She didn't know the word *depression*. Or at least didn't understand it could be an illness as much as a transient state of mind. People called her gloomy. Her mother used the word, "selfish".

"The phrase I remember hearing all the time," Deborah told me, "was *pull your bloody socks up*. Every fucking day. To the point where the words became meaningless. If only it was that simple."

She coped as best she could, found an aptitude for art at school.

"Landscapes," she said, "Always appealed to me. Must have been halfway through my fifth year, the art class went on a trip across the bridge to Fife," she said. "We stood at the edge of the road and looked over the water to the city. I loved the painting I made that day. Looking at it later, it would bring back the loneliness and isolation I felt looking across the water at all these buildings and people who lived so close to together. Know what my teacher told me?" She gritted her teeth as she spoke: "*Needs… More… Colour.*"

240

I thought back to the canvases I'd seen in the flat. Greys. Blacks. Stormy skies. Thickening shadows.

"I used to fantasize about killing myself," she said. "Dream about the patterns my blood would make. But I never went through with it. Thought it was some kind of growing-up thing, you know? Everyone felt like that even if they didn't admit it. Better to fool yourself into thinking that than accept the truth: that you're different. That you're... wrong."

Art college came next. The same teacher who told her she needed more colour supported her application.

"I loved it," Deborah said. "But I kept thinking... how can I afford this? Any of it."

Then she met Jennifer Furst.

Deborah's story tallied with Wickes's account and the details her sister had filled in for me. It was the emphasis that varied.

Like I said, ask three different people about the same events, you'll get three different versions.

"Do you ever think back, Mr McNee, on things you've done? Look at your past and see this person you don't recognise any more?"

I didn't answer her question.

I didn't want her to tell me the story she thought I wanted to hear.

I wanted the truth. Or as close as I could get.

"Maybe it's just me. Maybe the things I've done... they... I made mistakes. I know everyone does, but mine... I look back on that young woman and I can't always work out just what she was thinking. It's frightening sometimes. Because I can't say why I did everything I did. I can't understand myself." As she spoke, she wrapped her arms around her stomach as though to hold herself; a reassuring gesture. Her body was shaking gently, and I could feel sobs attempting to escape between words.

She told me about her repeated attempts to see Mary. How she started showing up at the Furst house, crashing family gatherings.

And then finally broke in at night to watch the baby sleeping.

"In my mind, I couldn't work out why they would be angry. Even if I was caught... if they could just see me, the way I was looking out for Mary, they'd maybe understand what the girl meant to me. Stupid, right?"

She wanted me to say it; "Aye."

Made her laugh, my agreeing so easily. I got the feeling she'd hadn't really laughed in a long time.

"Stupid girl," she said. "Really had a lot to learn." She kept reaching up towards her face. I knew what she was doing. Ex-smokers recognise their own. Can see those tell-tale gestures. The need for the release that cigarettes used to provide. All that unconscious play-acting; replicating comforting movements with none of the effects. "I keep wondering where things went wrong. When I reached the point of no return. I mean... was it... when I had Mary? When I agreed to the surrogacy? Or when I broke into their house. Think you can tell me that, Mr Detective? When did I mess it all up?"

Chapter 43

The first Deborah Brown knew of Wickes was a phone number scrawled on a piece of paper.

A friend had given it to her, telling her in no uncertain terms that she was in trouble. That this man could help her.

And she needed help. She knew it, then.

She needed a white knight.

Or she was going to die.

I asked, "How did your friend know Wickes?"

Deborah shook her head. Her gaze slipped to the floor. She swivelled one foot. A child-like gesture. "I don't know. This girl, she was in my class. She... I didn't have many friends, not really. She... she listened. I think he may have done some work for her dad, I don't know."

I let it go. It could slide for now, I figured. We'd get the full story once this situation was under control.

"I knew that in my heart. That unless someone took me away from everything, I was going to die. By my own hand. Or... someone else's."

Three nights after the incident where she broke

into the Furst household and watched their – *her* –
baby sleeping, she was woken from a light sleep by
someone banging on the door of her sister's place.
She'd been staying there since leaving the flat she'd
been sharing with other art students.

The reason for the move?

She told me, *personal issues.*

Given the rest of her story, that could have meant
anything.

"Couldn't have been past nine in the evening," she
said, talking about the banging on the door. She'd
been sleeping a lot in those days. For all she slept –
and with the black depression that was shrouding
her more than ever, she was sleeping a lot – she
never felt like she could get enough rest. She was
always tired, crawling back under the covers the
moment she tried to get up. The world was too much
for her. All she wanted was an escape.

I understood the feeling.

Wished I could reach out, let her know she wasn't
alone.

But I wasn't talking to her as a friend. Not as a
confidante or a sympathetic ear.

I was an investigator.

Searching for the truth. Couldn't afford to distort
it by throwing my own feelings into the mix.

Detachment. My professional watchword.

The one quality I strived for and rarely reached.

"They were ugly," she told me. "The two of them. I
remember that. One of them had stupid hair, looked
like Peter Stringfellow jacked out on steroids, you
know?" She laughed at little at the memory. "They
told me that I knew why they were there." And she
did, but claimed not to anyway; some tiny part of
her hoping they'd believe her, think they'd made a

mistake and just walk away.

Didn't happen of course.

The two of them beat her. Hard.

"They just walked right in. I tried to close the door, but they kicked it back. I remember stumbling back and closing my eyes. Opening them again and seeing this fist right in front of me. Then I didn't know what had happened until I was on the floor. They kicked me, you know? I couldn't help but remember when I was six years old and this boy thought it would be funny to punch me in the stomach. This older boy – Gary, that was his name, Gary Smith, I had such a crush on him – he stepped in and grabbed the other boy. Told him, you don't punch girls in the stomach. It's wrong. Plain wrong."

I remembered being told the same thing when I was young. Among the many sins you could commit – and given Scotland's Calvinist heritage, the litany of sins were a shared memory we all had of childhood – punching a girl in the stomach ranked somewhere just short of genocide.

The two thugs beat Deborah hard. Landed her in hospital. A broken wrist, shattered ribs and black eyes you couldn't disguise with just a pair of sunglasses like they did in the films.

She lied about what happened, of course. Knew that the attending doctors in the A&E didn't believe her. But then, she knew what would happen if she told the truth.

She made Kathryn keep quiet, too.

"It was our first real fight as sisters," she told me. "I mean, we fought over things when we were younger, but this was the first time it felt like maybe there was no way back from what either of us said that night. I'm amazed she ever talked to me again."

Say what you like about their methods, the hired muscle had made their point.

The worst part was that I knew David Burns wouldn't have given a fuck about the pain Deborah suffered. For all his grandiose talk of being a family man in touch with the people, he was a cold-hearted bastard who wouldn't blink twice at any atrocity committed in his name.

But, of course, he wasn't so cold hearted that he would get his own hands dirty. Oh, no. He was too much of a fucking coward for that.

***

Deborah told me she needed air.

I let her step out the back door. Everything was under control. We had time.

What was important: Mary was safe. We knew where she was. The ticking clock had turned mute.

Susan had been standing in the hallway. I didn't know for how long. She came in when Deborah went out the back door and reached out to place her hand on my arm. She squeezed gently.

"It's a mess, aye?"

I nodded.

She said, "Mary's fine. In case you were wondering."

It felt like a rebuke, although there was nothing in the way she spoke that came across as vicious.

I looked at the back door, which sat ajar.

"I'm glad."

"I heard what she was saying."

I nodded, kept looking at the door. "She never meant the girl any harm."

"But she has to understand –"

I cut Susan off, waving my hand. Didn't want to hear what she had to say.

"You talk a lot about being detached," she said. "How a good investigator never involves himself in the lives of his clients. How you sit back, refuse to let your emotions get the better of you. Great delusion, Steed. You're nothing but emotions. Why else did you stick with this case?"

I pretended that I hadn't heard. "She's scared for her daughter, you know."

"But scared of what? That business with Burns, if she hadn't come back –"

"That's not it."

"Then what?"

I'd taken my eyes from the door. Hadn't noticed Deborah come back inside.

She said, "His name is Wickes. And he's a killer. He was going to kill Mary. Because I loved her. Do you understand? I had to protect her."

***

Wickes.

Charming, empathetic and sweet. That's how Deborah described him. At least, her first impressions.

He came to her. She'd called that number, spoken to him and the next day he showed up at her door. Overnight train.

Who could resist a damsel in distress?

That was what he said. Patronising? Perhaps, but I knew what he was like, how his earnestness could make you believe almost anything he said.

He listened to her story without interruption. Didn't ask for clarification, justification or any of that bullshit. Took her at her word. When she was done, he said, "You don't deserve any of this."

She told him she didn't know why she'd called. Didn't know what he could do.

In the end, she asked him to help her escape. Not just Burns and his thugs, but her mess of a life. She needed to start over again. Hit the reset button. Give herself a second chance.

Maybe that was how she could get rid of this cloud that had hung over her for so long. The one she thought would be lifted when she had the child. When she worked her way into the affections of the Furst family. When she did something that might finally give her life the meaning she thought had been missing.

He did as she asked.

Because he was smitten.

"When he came through the door, he had this look like he'd just been hit on the head by a falling slate, you know? I thought he was handsome, too."

Deborah smiled at the memory. For a moment, all the worry that had gathered in her features seemed to melt away and I saw this look in her eyes that seemed innocent. A glimpse of who she used to be, perhaps.

Susan said, "This was the man you just called a killer? A psychopath?"

"Don't all the girls love the bad boys."

I didn't have to look at Susan to know she wasn't holding back the sneer.

"When did he change?" I asked.

Deborah looked at me, and that innocence that had momentarily overtaken her was again replaced by the hardness that she had grown into. She didn't appear older, exactly. Just tougher. The kind of woman who wasn't going to take shite from anyone anymore.

"He changed," she said, "Slowly. Or it seemed that way to me. Maybe I was just trying to fool myself. Who wants to admit, after all, that they've made that kind of mistake? That the man they find themselves falling in love with is just as likely to kill them as kiss them."

Susan said, "Tell us."

Chapter 44

He set her up in a one bedroom flat in Glasgow. Arranged protection. Made her feel safe.

"Any time I had doubts, he would tell me, 'this is the only way you can escape what's happened,' and I believed him."

There were rules, of course.

No old friends. No contact with family. No telling anyone about her past.

In the end, this boiled down to no talking to anyone without clearing it through him.

He became her constant companion.

At first she found it endearing. Necessary? Aye, she believed that he was with her at all times because he cared. He was protecting her.

When I had talked to Wickes about Deborah, he had harped on about her obsessive nature. Her fixation on people and things. He told me how she couldn't let anything go.

Psychologists have this word: *projection*.

"He hated me talking to anyone. We'd go out, I'd spend all my time with him. Anyone I talked to, I did more or less through him. He censored conversations. Friendships. Kept telling me I needed to be careful. And I believed him because I was young."

I said, "And because you were scared."

She nodded. Could barely look up at me and Susan, as though she was ashamed to admit the truth.

Soon enough, she was living with Wickes. In his house. And later, in his bed. Because it was easier. Because he had begun to convince her that she was in love with him. "I don't know how it happened," she said. "Maybe after long enough you become so used to the idea of someone being there that you think it's got to be love because why else would they always be around? Why else would you be thinking about them all the time? He wouldn't let me walk to the shops without him. I told him I needed some company that wasn't him. He bought me a dog."

I figured it was hardly proof he had a heart.

Although it fooled Deborah for a while.

The dog was named Chess, Deborah claimed after an uncle she had. Maybe his full name had been Chester, although that wasn't a typically Aberdonian name and she'd never thought to ask him.

Whatever the case, she loved Chess the dog; a dark-haired mongrel with a white streak that ran from above his eyes and along the back of his head. He used to love it when she tickled those light hairs and scratched at the skin underneath. His presence helped calm her down. She'd spend a lot of time with the dog outside in the back garden. He was not just a pet. He was – in her words – her confidante.

"Does that sound strange?" she asked us. "That my best friend in the world was a dog? That I told all

251

my secrets to someone who could never offer advice, who probably didn't even understand what I was saying?"

Chess seemed to calm the situation between her and Wickes. The arguments quit, and she began to think maybe things would get better. She was simply going through a period of adjustment.

As the months went by, Wickes stopped giving the dog so much attention, started telling Deborah how she was, "spoiling the mutt."

"Only when it got bad did I even realise how he'd changed," she said. "Slipped back into his old ways. He hated the damn dog. Used to tell me I was too lenient with Chess. Started saying how I loved it more than him. Never called the dog by his name. Always, *it*."

Susan asked, "Did you? Love the dog more than Wickes?"

Deborah hesitated. Reluctant to answer. Then: "Yes. But how hard was that? He'd been my white knight, and then... he became... I felt like a prisoner, you know? He would remind me every day how he had rescued me. I'd traded one fear for another."

"He frightened you?"

"When I broke the rules... or he felt I wasn't listening to him... He'd get this look in his eyes. As if something was popping back there in his brain. I could see the sparks; the fire. I used to think he was so sweet. And then some nights I'd find myself waking up, scared that I was going to find those big fucking hands round my throat. He was going to kill me, throw me away, because I wasn't being the girl he wanted me to be."

An unspoken question hung in the air: why didn't she just leave?

But it was a question Susan and I had asked many times before of so many different people. Working as coppers, we'd encountered victims of abuse who stayed in their situation because they were afraid that if they left things would become even worse. Why swap one hell for another?

The event that sealed the deal for Deborah was the death of the dog.

I remembered Wickes telling me about this. Deborah killing the dog rather than letting it be put down.

"We fought about it. He said I loved the dog more than him. Over and over, it became like a little joke in a way. A joke with a bad punch line, but the closest we had to one. I remember he came home one night, saw me feeding some of our dinner to Chess. Just a wee treat, you know? Sometimes you have to spoil them. I mean, where's the harm?"

Wickes didn't see things that way.

"I make him sound like a bastard. But... that was the first time he ever touched me," Deborah said.

The first time she realised fully what the man was capable of.

She'd traded one kind of fear for another. Her whole life defined by it.

As she spoke, her posture drooped and she cracked the knuckles on her right hand. "He grabbed me by the throat, pushed me against the wall. Told me that I should love him. What the fuck had the dog ever done for me?"

Susan asked, "This was the first time he attacked you?"

"Yes." Insistent, as though she was making a point. Maybe a part of her still felt bound to defend him in some fashion. He wasn't all bad. No one could

253

be, could they?

But she had always known that something like that night would happen. It was always there, in his attitude. The way he spoke to her. No overt threats, but something lurking beneath his words. Innuendo of the worst possible kind.

And that night she fed the dog scraps of their food, she realised that it was no misunderstanding. No joke.

"He said that maybe I'd appreciate him if the fucking dog just went away."

That night, she'd gone to bed frightened of when he would join her. She lay beneath the sheets with her fingers up at her throat, gently probing at the marks his fingers had left.

The next morning, she got up and he was gone.

She took the dog out to the back garden.

Thought about leaving.

Watched the dog lap up water from the bowl.

If she walked, could he find her? Would he simply forget her?

That day, the sun was high in the sky. Mid July, she remembered. A Monday. Where they lived, the city would sometimes be still and it was possible to ignore the distant sounds of traffic that had kept her awake when she first moved into that tiny flat that Wickes had arranged for her. His own place, she told us, was removed. Isolated.

The dog, Chess, lapped at the water in his bowl with the kind of absolute concentration dogs reserve specially for such occasions. You'd believe that he hadn't had anything to drink in days to watch the way he gulped it down.

Deborah stood by the door, her mind drifting on other thoughts but always conscious of the throbbing at the base of her throat where Wickes's hands had squeezed the tightest. Some breaths came harder than others, and she began to worry that maybe something inside her throat had been damaged. She reached up, traced the outline of the bruises with the ends of her fingers.

Watched the dog.

As Chess looked up from his bowl and straight at her.

"It was like this final understanding passed between us," she said. "I knew something was wrong, even if for a second he looked so perfectly normal. Absolutely calm. Just… looking at me."

The dog pitched on his side suddenly, as though his legs had just stopped working. He started making a strange sound, a high pitched keening that sounded so utterly absurd and alien it took Deborah a moment to realise that it was coming from Chess.

"I didn't know what was happening. His legs started kicking and he started foaming at the mouth. I remember thinking… Rabies. The only thing I could think that could cause something like that. But it wasn't. He'd have been angry, aye? Dangerous. Chess wasn't any of that. He was in pain. I think as confused by what was happening as I was."

The dog was dead in minutes.

When she made to go back in the house to call the police, Wickes was waiting for her. Standing in the kitchen with this strange expression on his face that she couldn't quite read.

She exploded.

Wanted to kill him. Grab one of the kitchen knives, slit the big bastard's throat. All his talk of protecting her, and he killed the one thing that –

She never got the chance.

He beat her wordlessly. Not even a laugh. "That's when he's at his most dangerous," she said, "When he goes quiet."

"When he was done, he dragged me into the hall and threw me in the cupboard beneath the stairs. There was a lock on the outside of that door, and I'd never questioned why. I thought he was going to lock me in there. In the dark. Alone."

I remembered Wickes's version of events, felt my muscles start to tense. Tasted bile in my mouth.

After a while in the dark, she remembered the door opening. Thought that he had come to his senses, that he was going to let her out. She imagined – briefly – a tearful apology, and a promise that this kind of thing would never happen again.

He loved her. Never wanted to hurt her.

What happened was nowhere close to her romantic dream.

He threw the dog's corpse in there with her.

Locked the door.

Left her overnight with the dead dog.

As Deborah told us her story, I reached out and touched Susan's arm. Felt the anger buzzing through her. If Wickes had been there at that moment, I doubt he would have lived too long.

I thought about Wickes's version of events, how convincing he had seemed to me at the time. I had to wonder: did he believe his own lies? Over time had he deluded himself that his version of events was the truth?

Could that excuse in any way the things that he had done?

After the death of Chess and the assault, all of

Deborah's fight left her. Rather than allowing her to be free, Wickes had trapped her. She had no control over her life. He had the final say over everything she did. He decided whether her life was worth living.

"When you realise that, when you realise that it's all utterly hopeless, something inside you snaps. You give in. You surrender yourself to the world. What can it do to you now that it hasn't already?"

The dog had been his message. She'd heard it loud and clear.

I looked across at Susan, who had edged away from my touch.

Her jaw had set tight. Her muscles were taut.

Whether her anger was for the dog or Deborah, I wasn't entirely sure.

Chapter 45

The death of the dog changed everything.

"I know it sounds strange," she said, "but until he killed Chess, I believed he loved me."

For all the things he did to her, she said, she still saw something human in him.

When he brought Chess into the house, it was the last time she believed that he would do anything out of the goodness of his heart.

"I was paralysed after that night. If he could do that to the dog... what could he do to me?"

It was a recurring pattern. Every time she found some connection outside of Wickes, he took it away from her. His insistence that she sever all ties with family and friends. The way he put the kibosh on any friendships she might have made when they went out.

After Wickes killed Chess, he didn't need to lock the doors. Deborah stayed inside.

"I didn't want to go anywhere. I just wanted to die."

Two nights after the dog's death, she took a knife

from the kitchen, tried opening her wrists. Failed. The marks were still on her arms, pink ridges on her otherwise smooth skin. "I don't think they'll ever go away."

Like the worst kind of memories.

Any normal person would have rushed her to hospital. Wickes took care of her himself.

"After that, he appeared to show genuine remorse. Kept telling me how he did everything that he did for my safety. How I was all that mattered to him in the world."

Susan said, "Did you believe him?" Her voice harsh.

Deborah hesitated before saying anything. "I don't know."

After the suicide attempt, the balance shifted again. Wickes encouraged her to rekindle her painting. Wanted her to find a hobby. Anything to keep her interested.

Soon enough, he relaxed his rules.

Guilt? Maybe.

For all his psychosis, I couldn't help thinking about the look he got in his eyes when he talked about Deborah. His face would soften in a fashion that's hard to fake. I genuinely believed that he thought he was in love with her.

"I might have loved him again," Deborah said. "But the dog... I couldn't stop thinking about Chess lying there on the ground, his body shaking and his mouth foaming. His eyes... I remember him looking up at me... and I couldn't help thinking he was asking me why this was happening. What he had done to deserve a death like this."

It worried Deborah, haunted her dreams at night.

"I would wake up, feeling like there was a weight

pressing down on me. On my chest. And I knew it was Chess, that the bastard had gone and dug up his wee corpse, that's he'd thrown the dead dog in bed with me for a laugh. There was never anything there, of course."

I knew there wasn't, but the fear was so potent that her nightmares would seem real to her even after waking. I understood that.

But what the incident with Chess had done to destroy any trust between them was to make her worry what he would do if he ever discovered the one secret she had managed to keep from him.

***

"You can't walk away from your own child. Your flesh and blood. It's impossible. You can talk about it all you want, but in the end, you'll wind up missing them. There'll be a hole in your life. And you can ignore it. Refuse to acknowledge it. But it'll be there. In one form or another, and I don't think anyone will ever be able to fill it entirely." Deborah looked away from Susan to me. "I don't know if it's different for men. Or if it's just me. But Mary was part of me for nine months. We shared a body. We shared things that she could never have with that – with Jennifer Furst. You can't just let that go."

Even when Wickes told her what she stood to lose if she retained any contact at all with her family, her friends, her daughter, she couldn't just let go so easily.

And the way she looked at the arrangement, she was allowed one secret. How could it matter if you retained a link with someone who didn't even know who you were?

260

She had a photograph.

Taken from the Furst family home. Sneaked inside her pocket that night she broke in.

In the bothy's kitchen, she pulled that photograph out from the rear pocket of her jeans and unfolded it: battered and lined and faded with the years. But none of that mattered.

Mary had been a beautiful baby, in a white dress with a lace collar, pictured against the background of a family Christmas. The tree and the presents in the background. She was surrounded by ripped and crumpled wrapping paper, smiling as she hugged her new toy; a large white dog with big black eyes and a felt tongue that hung loose from its dumbly gaping mouth.

"I showed this picture to Mary. She said she had the dog until she turned ten and then she lost it somewhere. She doesn't remember where. She called it Glen. Doesn't know where the name came from. Maybe Jennifer gave it to her. Maybe it was just a word that stuck, aye? Who knows?" Deborah smiled as she handed us the picture to look at. Again, the kind of smile I had difficulty ever imagining Jennifer Furst using when she thought about her daughter.

What had Susan said earlier about my getting emotionally involved?

Both Susan and I dutifully examined the image and passed it on. It wasn't important to us. But Deborah needed for us to look as though there might be something in that image that would make us understand everything.

Maybe I wanted to see it, too.

She needed us to be on her side. It had been so long since anyone had taken the time to truly listen to and understand her that she was desperate to make her feelings known; reaching out for anyone who might empathise with her.

I wanted to pull her close and tell her that everything was going to work out. But I didn't.

Couldn't.

Part of Wickes's makeup plan had been to offer Deborah the chance to apply for an art course at a local college. She'd never completed her degree at Duncan of Jordanstone back in Dundee. And Wickes understood the need for her to feel she had some freedom. It wasn't that he was without heart, but he understood the kind of difficulties he would face without taking some kind of affirmative action.

The kindest acts sometimes come from the cruellest place.

She took the offer, under a series of strict rules. Similar to those imposed on her when she first moved in with him.

Deborah started to convince herself that Wickes was calming down.

The incident with Chess had been a one-off. Oh, aye, he didn't mean it. Just had a mean temper. And forget that, look at all that he had done to help her.

He was her saviour, right?

Wasn't that what she wanted?

Wasn't that what he told her?

He wouldn't do anything that wasn't in her best interests.

Easy to think that when the bruises began to fade. When the memory of that night in the cupboard, huddled together with the corpse of a poisoned dog began to fade like the worst nightmares always do.

A few months after she started, she went out for a swift drink with someone she'd met on the course. A young guy – young enough she wasn't that interested in him – with a good line in jokes who didn't seem to take himself quite as seriously as some of the others in the class.

A drink was all she was after. A drink in someone else's company. Without the Big Man's presence looming over here.

She had a good night, too. Until the guy went to the bathroom. Never came back.

That was when Wickes sat down across the table from her, this grin on his face like he knew something she didn't.

"A child with a guilty secret," she said. "He could look like that, sometimes, when he'd done the most terrible things." Stumbling again. Dancing around the edges of her life with Wickes had become second nature. She knew that he had done terrible things. But when it came to the specifics, perhaps there was still some of that old fear left in her. If she talked about it, admitted the truth, she knew what he could do. What he *would* do. "I knew something had happened. I didn't… I mean… I thought that he'd gone over the edge. Killed that lad. Just for talking to me, you know?"

When they went home at the end of the night, Wickes acted as though nothing had happened.

The next morning, she went to class as usual. The guy wasn't there.

"He ever turn up?"

Deborah looked surprised at Susan's question. The answer should have been obvious. "I asked the course convener about it, why he hadn't come back. She said she'd talked to him, some kind of personal issue meant he wasn't able to continue the course."

The call meant that Wickes hadn't killed the man.

Deborah could cling to that, at least. Getting roughed up was better than winding up dead. But the message from Wickes was clear: he was all she ever needed.

That was when she began to worry for Mary. That night brought everything into focus for her.

Funny the way the brain works sometimes, the connections that it makes. How one incident can lead you to see another – unconnected – in a whole new light.

She'd kept that picture of Mary. Her one betrayal.

It had seemed insignificant at the time.

Would Wickes see it like that?

When she graduated, Deborah applied for a teaching course. Again, Wickes loosened her leash.

The "leash" metaphor was apt. She felt like a pet; a dumb animal who couldn't look after herself. That was how he treated her, how she sometimes came to think of herself.

Her world became defined by praise or condemnation from this bastard. Any disobedience was punished. Any glimmer of independent idea was squashed.

Her only rebellion: the photograph.

A baby on Christmas morning.

Her baby.

What might have been.

She enjoyed the freedom she was allowed. Took to the teaching job with enthusiasm and dedication. Was careful to avoid socialising with other members of staff, became aware of her reputation as talented but cold. Figured she was protecting everyone else, didn't care what they thought of her for it.

I remembered Ms Foster telling me how Deborah had rarely socialised with any other teachers at the school. How when she came close to talking about anything personal, she would leave or change the subject.

She was a martyr. Suffered in silence.

Something romantic in that, or so she started to tell herself.

Every night, she locked herself in the bathroom, looked at that picture.

Imagined the girl that the baby had grown into.

Knew what Wickes would do if he discovered the truth. If he knew what she was thinking.

"The teaching gave me a way out," she said. "While I was in school, I was out of his sight for a while. I felt relaxed. I felt… like me again."

I asked, "When did you think about tracking down your daughter?"

"I heard about an opening in Dundee. Knew that I would be stupid to come back. But all the same… fifteen years. Who would remember me, right? And just to have that connection –" She stopped talking for a moment, and I thought maybe she wouldn't be able to go on. She had been talking for almost twenty minutes, only the occasional interruption from me or Susan.

Then: "He thought that I was his. That he owned me. And maybe he did, but as long as I had the picture… I don't know, if he had taken that away from me, maybe things would have been different. The picture gave me hope. Reminded me that there was something I wanted outside of the world that he defined for me. I couldn't just walk away, of course. And I knew I had to be careful. Had to make him believe that he had won. That he had broken me completely." She took several deep breaths, as though she was about to duck her head beneath water with no idea when she would come back to the surface. "Took me a long time, but I had him convinced. I started taking more chances. He started to look at me less intently, believing that I was too scared to do anything that would upset him."

That was when she got back in touch with her sister. Kathryn helped her to set up an escape, helped her with the move back to Dundee.

"I was away. He didn't know where I'd gone. I left nothing behind."

Wickes had told me that it had only been the last few weeks he realised something was wrong, made it sound like he'd come here the minute he realised something was wrong.

"I was here for months. He talks a good game, Mr McNee but in the end he didn't help me disappear like he promised. He just isolated me from the world. Made me afraid. He talks like he could hunt anyone to the ends of the earth, but that's all it is. Talk. He's full of hot fucking air. Only thing he can do well is hurt people."

But even if he wasn't so smart as he liked to make out, he still tracked her down. "I heard there was someone asking around about me. A few of my colleagues at the school, they said that some bearded guy had been asking how well they knew me, where I lived, if they had my number. Because we'd been on a few dates and he's lost my contact details."

That had been when she'd realised what was happening. She'd already told Mary the truth, made the girl promise not to tell anyone. It was their secret. But now, she had to be sure that the girl trusted her. Because if the incident with Chess had taught her anything about Wickes, it was that he didn't care who or what he hurt.

266

Or killed.

"I panicked. I mean, I thought maybe if we came out here, I don't know, we could figure out something... It was stupid, I know. But who else was going to protect her from that bastard?"

Susan said. "The police."

Deborah laughed. No humour. Hard and cynical. "Don't take this personally, but –" She stopped talking, lifted her head.

The sound of an engine outside.

She looked at me, "You said no one else –"

"They don't."

The engine cut off.

I looked at Susan. She shook her head. Not her doing.

The sound of a car door slamming shut.

I knew who it was out there.

Looking at Deborah, I could see she knew it, too.

Chapter 46

Deborah pushed past us, into the front room. Hustled Mary back out. Looked at me and said, "Keep her safe."

I nodded.

Susan looked at Deborah, said, "He knew about Mary, didn't he? Figured out what you were doing?"

Deborah nodded. "That's why I had to protect her. He would have killed her. To teach me a lesson."

Mary remained silent throughout all of this, sticking it out in the front room, watching the TV snow and insulating herself from everything that was happening.

The big question: why did Mary trust Deborah Brown so implicitly? This woman who claimed to be her mother. Who hadn't seen Mary since she was a baby.

The girl everyone had talked about when I started making enquiries had been smart and sensitive and popular. But the biggest clue probably came from Jennifer Furst:

The last few years, it's like she's been looking for

herself. It's something I can't help her with. I don't know if anyone can.

I think she had known instinctively that the woman who raised her was not a blood relative.

Did she know the truth when she met this Deborah? Walking into art class for the first time, did she get hit with some bolt of lightning? Did she realise that somehow this woman could help her find out who she was?

What made her trust Deborah enough to simply vanish with her?

There had been no coercion. No forcing the issue.

Maybe that's how it is with family.

An instinctive trust borne through the blood.

Some families, perhaps.

Others have to work at it.

I didn't have the answers. Maybe never would. Sometimes, to get at the heart of someone's story, you have to be so much inside their head that you can understand the incommunicable motivations that drive them. So many decisions we make are inarticulate, leaving us isolated and alone in our actions and choices.

Deborah and Mary were in the kitchen. They'd locked the back door.

Susan and I stood near the front door.

I heard the sound of heavy footsteps crunching on frost outside.

Susan looked at me.

The door rattled. Then someone started hammering with their fists. Howling. A strange, heightened sound; barely human.

The cry of a predator.

Or a madman.

Susan turned back and said to Deborah. "You've

got a phone?"

"No."

There had been no lines leading to the house.

"Christ! I can't get reception here. You've got to have stayed in touch with your sister, someh –"

"A box about two miles away. Main street of a wee hamlet. I walked down there once every day, called my sister. Seemed safer than –"

"Open the fucking door!"

Wickes. His voice guttural, shredding his vocal chords with anger.

Susan looked to me again, took a deep breath and then turned to the door. "This is Detective Constable Bright of Tayside Constabulary," she said, her voice strong and assured.

Aye, you don't mess with Detective Susan.

"I am asking you to step away from the door, get back in your car and drive away."

"Fucking bitch!"

"I'm giving you one warning –"

He didn't want to listen to her. "You in there, McNee? Did the cunt give you the sob story about how badly I treated her? She needed protecting, you know. From the world. Herself. You understand? How people need saving? From themselves as much as anyone. You know we're alike, McNee. Both of us. We understand people. What they need. We step up to help them when no one else will."

I didn't say anything.

My muscles contracted. My fists closed. Blood beat around in my skull.

I closed my eyes. Felt that pressure inside my head. Same as when I'd woken after cracking my head on the concrete.

My legs felt unbalanced.

I could have toppled over.

All I heard was his voice. Echoing around, bouncing off the bones of my skull. "The thing is, you know it, we're easily led, McNee. You and me. So fuckin' desperate to help people, they take advantage. I know what she's told you. The things she said. The fuckin' lies. Come on, pal, who the fuck do you believe? We're brothers in arms." He hammered on the door again. The wood was shaking, buckling. Could he break through? Man his size, I wasn't sure.

"The cunt's a fuckin' liar!"

Susan turned back to look at me.

I stepped forward.

She said, "The thing about going to CID, it's all head-work. The thinking copper's game. Been a while since I'd had to sort out a brawl." She smiled.

"Like riding a bike," I said.

The banging stopped.

Susan reached out, touched my forearm.

A small gesture. And like everything else in life, it was fleeting.

Susan said, her voice unnaturally loud in the sudden silence, "Think he's given up?"

"You?"

"Aye, right."

Something started smacking on the door. A different kind of sound. Not fists and feet.

The wood splintered.

I remembered. Outside. The axe. Rusty and unused, but a weapon all the same.

The wood panels splintered in.

"Here's fuckin' Johnny!" A howl. A roar. No: a war cry.

Susan said, "This is your last chance, Mr Wickes —"

271

Like anything we said could have made a difference.

The door crashed in.

He was bigger than I remembered; maybe the shadows or my imagination. The adrenaline.

His eyes were wild, and those hands could have crushed someone's skull.

To Susan: "Do you ever shut the fuck up?"

Susan said, "Put down the axe." Her tone even and measured. I remembered her talking about attending the crisis negotiation skills workshop a few months back. Hoped they taught more than hot air.

Wickes stepped forward. Moving fast, swinging round with the axe. In the narrow corridor there was nowhere for Susan to move.

I couldn't react fast enough.

Again. Something in this man made me react in a primal fashion; the prey's reaction to the presence of a predator.

The blade arced in a blur.

Susan appeared to move before it struck her. Her body jerking, her head snapping back and her arms flailing.

Took me a moment to realise Wickes had managed to strike her with the butt of the axe. The handle. Right in the face.

But it wasn't the business end.

Susan crumpled fast. I ran forward. Not thinking, just wanting to grab the fucker's throat, squeeze the life out of him.

The world blurred around the edges. That sound of the ocean in my head grew even louder, the bass line of my pulse sounding just below that constant roar. Made me feel lighter than air; I could fucking fly.

The axe swung.

I ducked, thinking I was too slow, marvelling it never hit me, heard the head smash into the wall.

I came up underneath, hoped to fuck it was stuck. And...

He doesn't waste a moment. Lets go of the axe, brings both hands round on either side of my head and slams them together.

Chapter 47

I couldn't move.

Paralysed?

The word echoed in my brain. Took on its own weight, forced my head back down onto the uncarpeted floorboards.

He'd cracked the base of my skull with those sledgehammer hands, caught me beneath the ear.

There are tiny bones in the ear that help with balance and co-ordination. What happens if they get broken?

My body was heavy, sluggish. A burden.

My neck screamed in protest as I turned to see where he'd gone.

How long had I been lying there?

All I could think was: *I've failed. Again.*

The over-arching pattern of my life.

Who was I kidding thinking anything had changed over the last year? Was I somehow a better person because I could pretend to be at peace with what had happened to Elaine? Because I no longer spent my time trying to figure just how it was my fault that someone I loved had died?

His footsteps echoed back along the floor. His voice – dulled and unclear through the cotton wool that had clogged my brain – roared threats like some animal closing in for the kill.

I needed to move.

I closed my eyes, concentrated, rolled over, made it onto my stomach. Let out a cry from the effort and stayed still for a few seconds to regain my strength. Enough at least to raise my head.

I could see back into the kitchen. Mary was slumped against the units, her body loose, her head lolling to one side. Blood dripping from her nose.

Dead?

Oh Jesus, after all this, dead?

I flexed my hands, pressed down and tried to lift myself off the floor.

A couple of inches. My muscles trembling.

I collapsed again.

Vomited.

The bile burned my throat and the back of my nose. Threatening to choke me. Talk about undignified. But no one dies like a hero. Not in real life.

My skull was vibrating. My vision was blurred. My muscles ached, unwilling to work for me.

A punch to the head.

After everything that had happened, I could die because some prick gave me a sucker punch to the head?

My eyes were blazing. On fucking fire.

I looked at Mary.

Her right hand twitched.

She was alive.

She was alive.

I lifted my head. Blinked out the blur.

Fuck this.

I wasn't going out. I wasn't giving up.

I swallowed hard. My ears popped.

The sounds of the outside world rushed into my skull. Tried to knock me down again.

"This is on your fucking head. Do you understand? All of this is your fault!" Wickes. Not talking to me. I guessed he was talking to Deborah. Out of sight behind the kitchen doorway. Punctuating every word with a dull thump. Sounded like he was hammering a head of lettuce.

My stomach churned.

Fuck this self pitying crap.

I reached out, grabbed the wall. Hauled myself to my feet.

Didn't look behind me. Told myself that Susan was fine. She'd rip me a new arsehole if I attended to her first.

Aye, protect the innocent first and foremost.

My left leg was useless. The old wound playing up. As though the muscles had snapped. I imagined them like pressured strings on a guitar, tensed to breaking point.

I roared.

Struggled.

Hands on the walls to steady myself.

My eyes on Mary.

That one hand clenching. Eyes flickering. As though she wanted to wake up, couldn't quite figure it out.

I pushed the walls for momentum.

The rhythmic thumping from the kitchen pulled me along.

Through the door, I stopped, one hand on the wall, barely able to keep upright when I saw the source of

276

the noise.

Wickes had a grip on Deborah's hair. Her body was limp, legs bent at the knees, spine curved. Her arms flailed, useless, and for a moment I might have convinced myself that the big bastard had a grip on some kind of rubber doll.

Smashing her face against the worktop.

The veins popped out on his neck. His skin flushed red, his eyes bulged.

His movements were brutal yet mechanical. I couldn't say for sure if he even knew what he was doing.

One last thump and he stopped.

Let go. Looked up at me.

Loosened that grip.

Deborah dropped.

No resistance.

Her head smacked against the worktop, bounced off the floor once and then she was completely still.

Blood pooled.

"Think she gets it," he said. "She understands."

He was trembling.

Remorse?

Was this fucking monster even capable of such a thing?

He said, "I loved her, you know. Believe it, McNee. I loved her."

"You killed her."

He said nothing.

"You killed her." The repetition no longer for his benefit. I felt empty, as though something had been stolen from me. My voice threatened to crack. I swallowed, turned my full attention onto him. "Because she loved her daughter? Because she didn't want to be yours alone?"

My legs were shaking. I could feel the world spinning on its axis.

How long could I stand?

If he turned on me, could I fight back?

"You didn't love her, you fuck. You wanted to possess her. If she couldn't be yours, she couldn't be anyone's, right? That's why you killed the dog."

Wickes said, "Natural fucking causes," in this low and uncertain voice. A child who knew he was going to be caught in a lie.

"You really believe that?" My leg was still on fire, but the pain had become dull and distant.

He didn't say anything. Looked down at the body on the floor.

The inside of my head was roaring.

"It didn't have to be like this," he said. "It wasn't supposed to be like this."

I said, "You were supposed to protect her."

He nodded. Took deep breaths.

Looked ready to collapse himself.

"It's over, then," I said. "All of this. Done with."

He got down on his knees, reached out towards Deborah, touched the back of her head with the tips of his fingers. Caressed her hair, matted with blood.

He started crying like he didn't know how this had happened. Was at a loss to explain any of it.

Chapter 48

Wickes was still in the kitchen, cuffed to the boiler. We hadn't moved him far.

We'd left Deborah's body alone. Susan figured it was best to touch as little around the scene as possible. Let the SOCO crew deal with it. Give them an uncontaminated scene to work with.

"We're going to have to answer a lot of questions."

I was hoisting Mary's body off the floor. She was breathing, maybe a little shallow, but she was going to live. The plan was to get her in the front room, make her comfortable.

I said to Susan, "If I've learned how to do one thing the past year, it's answer questions from the police."

Sounded flippant even to me.

Wickes had gone silent on us. Was it possible he had never been able to acknowledge the things he had done? That when faced with the consequences of his actions, all he could do was shut down?

I figured him for playing some kind of con game.

Pleading insanity. Trying for a cushy sentence.

Solicitors would be lining up around the block to take a high profile case, and this one was going national.

Connolly was going to have my balls when he found out what had happened. He was going to be pissed off that he wasn't in on a scoop like this.

I wasn't happy about moving Mary, but I needed to get her away from the kitchen. Didn't want her to see what had happened to her mother. Gingerly, I lifted her, carried her through to the front room, laid her in the recovery position and placed my jacket over her for warmth. Mild concussion? Couldn't be sure. Not until the ambulance arrived.

Susan's nose had been broken. She said she was fine, but I noticed a slight distance in the way she talked. And her voice sounded thick, bunged up like a bad head cold. Looking at her pupils, I couldn't be sure, but I thought they seemed larger than usual.

I tried to figure how long it would take the ambulance to arrive.

And kept telling myself, it could have been worse.

When I'd first got to my feet in the hall, frustration and anger had been burning me from the inside out. The white hot needles in my brain had made me focus on nothing more than simple revenge.

For Susan.

I'd already seen someone I cared for die.

Someone I loved.

Already let the person responsible disappear. Let them get away with it.

It wasn't going to happen again.

When I confronted Wickes, ready to kill the man, to have the revenge I'd convinced myself I needed...

I couldn't do it.

I'd felt sorry for the bastard.

Imagine that; feeling pity for a fucking monster

like Wickes. A man who kept the woman he loved like a prisoner. Killed her dog. Tortured her psychologically and physically.

After making sure that Mary was comfortable, I went out into the hall with Susan. She stepped out of the shattered front door and into the night. Looked up at the stars.

Her feet crunched on the thin layer of night time frost. Her breath misted in the freezing air.

I stood behind her.

"You need to sit down," I said.

"We have to call someone."

I nodded, looked at the car. "She said the payphone was, what, maybe a mile or two?"

Susan nodded.

"You think you're okay to keep on that bastard back there?" I jerked my head back towards the house. Meaning Wickes.

"I don't think he'll be trouble."

I grunted, non-committal. I'd seen the way his attitudes and behaviour could change. "I can get a signal before then, I'll call."

"Steed, you need to sit down yourself." Susan placed both hands on either side of my face. Her skin was warm, and I wanted to close my eyes, just fall forward and collapse into her.

She said, "Your pupils are dilated."

Saying, *concussion* without mentioning the word.

The crashing waves in my skull had quit. I felt fine. Unsteady, but I figured I was okay to drive.

I'd rest soon enough.

What choice did we have? I wasn't taking him back in the car. Not with a dead body and both Susan and Mary in the state they were in. We needed coppers. We needed paramedics.

281

I'd take the car, head out, get a signal on the phone. Let them know where we were. What had happened.

Finally, I accepted this was something I couldn't handle alone.

And when I opened my eyes again and looked at Susan, I realised something.

I wasn't handling it alone.

***

I used to have nightmares. Dreaming of enclosed spaces. Blood. The still aftermath of the long scream of violence.

I would see faces I knew.

And I wouldn't know them, twisted as they were by the sight of blood and death.

When I woke up from these nightmares, I'd roll over and puke in the plastic tub I'd learned to keep beside the bed.

***

The bile gathered.

Susan was slumped in the hall near the kitchen, her legs bent up towards her chest, her head in her hands. Blood on her clothes.

I'd been gone maybe twenty minutes. Got the signal. Made the call. They were on their way.

It was over.

Except, I came back to...

What the fuck had happened?

I knelt beside Susan. She was breathing. Shallow. But she was alive.

I dropped the phone. It clattered to the wooden floor.

Said, "Mary?"

282

Susan looked up at me and nodded to the kitchen. "In there," she said.

I walked into the kitchen.

Deborah was still discarded on the floor.

Wickes was next to her.

The axe was buried in his chest. Didn't even look like he'd tried to ward off the attack. When I'd left he'd been close to comatose, had to wonder if maybe when the attack came he just no longer cared. One arm was stretched out, his palm resting gently on the small of Deborah's back. The gesture seemed bizarrely tender considering everything I knew about the man.

The floor was slick with blood.

And Mary was sitting against the back door, looking at the corpses.

Blood on her hands. The IPod I'd seen earlier in the front room plugged into her ears. I could hear the tinny sound of music emanating from the tiny speakers.

She had it turned up loud.

Drowning out the world.

She hummed with the music. The notes coming out in a halting fashion. She wasn't really thinking about what she was doing. Just trying to comfort herself.

As I came through the door, she stopped the humming, looked up at me and said, "He had to die. You understand, don't you? For what he did."

I took a breath. The air tasted tart, something coppery there. Maybe the blood. Maybe my imagination. I heard sirens.

Chapter 49

Mary was unresponsive after that. When I helped her to her feet, she took my outstretched hands with a kind of welcoming gratitude and allowed herself to be led back to the front room where she sat on the sofa again and started to shiver. I went to the bedroom and grabbed a blanket to put around her shoulders. Better than my jacket.

Susan and I talked in the hall, kept the door open so we could see Mary.

"So what do we do?"

I took a deep breath. "We can't let her take the blame for this. She's... she's been through a lot. I don't think –"

"We lie?"

"Bend the truth."

"How?"

"I killed Wickes. Self defence. After he killed Deborah, he was coming back for you and me. I finished him off."

"I had him cuffed to the radiator."

"So we uncuff him. You have a better story?"

She looked ready to say something, then cut herself off at the last minute. Spun around on her heels and punched out against one of the walls.

"You were in deep water last year, Steed. When they thought you killed that man at the Necropolis."

"I did kill him."

"In fear for your own life."

I didn't say anything.

Susan hesitated for a second, tried to catch my eyes as though she might see something in them.

I wasn't sure she'd see anything she liked.

"The story works if I attacked him," I said. "Can't think of anyone on the force would question that."

"And what about your business? I know you were on thin ice with the Association and the Security Council."

I looked through into the front room at the girl with the tattered blanket round her shoulders, her music blaring, her body shivering.

"Sometimes you have to make the sacrifice," I said, finally meeting her eyes. "We need to be together on this."

She hesitated.

"Forget our friendship," I said. "If we don't agree on what happened tonight –"

"And what about Mary?" asked Susan, her voice insistent.

"I don't – I think she'll stick with the story. I think she'll want to forget this. Go back to her life. Look at her."

Susan did, peering through the door.

I said, "If I was her, I'd take any opportunity to erase this night." When Susan turned back to look at me, I said, "Wouldn't you?"

***

DCI Ernie Bright acted the professional in front of his men.

Had them clear up while he walked us to a cop car. We leaned against the body while he smoked a cigarette, tried to think of something to say.

Caught between professionalism and fatherly concern.

I noticed one of the coppers trying to talk to Mary as he led her out to a waiting car. She wasn't saying a word. Hadn't uttered a sound since she told me that Wickes deserved that axe in the back of the neck.

Ernie said, "Two bodies. The kitchen looks like a slaughterhouse."

"The big bastard," I said. "He killed Deborah Brown. The woman."

Ernie nodded. "And who killed him?"

I hesitated.

Susan was standing beside me. Hadn't said a word since her father showed up.

I remembered our conversation in the car coming over here.

Would she bring that up here?

I was willing her to stick to the script as we'd agreed. Someone had to take the blame. Who could shoulder the responsibility. Knew enough of guilt that they could shoulder someone else's as well.

I started to open my mouth.

Susan said, "I did, sir."

It was the *sir* that got me.

But I think it hit Ernie even worse.

***

I stood near the overgrown area that might once

have been a vegetable garden. I could see the remains of canes and some signs of what might once have been an attempt to tame the weeds.

Ernie came and stood beside me.

I said, "She's giving a statement?"

"To another officer. I can't be involved."

I nodded. "Of course."

"DI Lindsay will take charge of this investigation." He shrugged. "Wish it could have been someone else, but there we are." He was dancing around something else. I waited for him to finally get to the point. "So tell me... would she lie to protect you?"

"No," I said. The lie came easy. But we'd both agreed: once the story was out, we would stick to it.

"Did you tell her about our little encounter the other day?"

I couldn't say anything to that.

"Something in her face, McNee. She's a good copper, and grand at the old bluff. But she could never fool her dad." He seemed ready to smile at that, but dropped it fast before it was fully formed.

I hesitated for just a moment before I said, simply, "She's your daughter. If you talk to her –"

"She's my daughter," he said. "And there are some things I don't think I'll ever be able to explain to her."

***

The next morning I woke up late, buried beneath heavy covers, feeling strangely detached from the world. I put my feet out on to the floor, stretched and tried to figure if I could separate the disjointed dreams from what had really happened.

I stumbled to the bathroom and looked at myself in the mirror.

Couldn't say what looked back at me.

Not with any certainty.

***

"Tell me, son, what separates us from them."

Three weeks before the accident that killed Elaine. Drinking with Ernie Bright at the Phoenix Bar on the Perth Road, tucked into a corner booth. A pep talk, if you like. He was fond of what he called informal training. Teaching the stuff the textbooks can't or won't.

"Honesty, son," he said. "Honesty and standards. All that good stuff." He smiled as he talked.

Looking back, I had to wonder if he believed it. Convinced himself of his own version of the truth? Because he was still hip deep with Burns and his crew in those days. A sacrifice of his principles for the greater good?

Smelled like shite to me.

"A good copper doesn't have to lie or cheat to get what he wants. Or to stoop to the level of the criminal, you understand? He's better than that. Appearances count."

Don't they just?

***

Something had been slipped under my door.

An envelope.

I tore it open to look inside. Photocopied police reports. A transcript. One I didn't want to read.

***

Present at interview:
Mary Furst
DC Dorothy Shepherd
DCI Ernie Bright
Also present: Rebecca Simpson (supporter)

Mary was a minor in the eyes of the law. No matter how mature she might appear there were guidelines that dictated how they would interview her. At least one female copper, hence the inclusion of DC Shepherd who would lead the interview. And a supporter; an independent party to oversee the interview. In this case, Rebecca Simpson was a social worker assigned by the council to Mary Furst's case. It could have been Jennifer, but Mary was refusing to speak to the woman who had raised her.

I could only imagine what was going through the girl's head.

DC SHEPHERD: *In your own words, Mary, I need you to tell us how Ms Brown made contact with you.*
MARY: *Contact?*
DC SHEPHERD: *How did she make herself known to you?*
MARY: *She was my art teacher.*
DC SHEPHERD: *That's not the whole truth, is it?*
MARY: *I didn't. No one told me the truth.*
DC SHEPHERD: *We're not here to talk about that. That's a matter –*
DCI BRIGHT: *For another time. A private conversation with her parents. Who I still think –*
MARY: *They're not my parents.*
DC SHEPHERD: *But they brought you up. They raised you.*

289

MARY: She was my teacher. I liked her. She listened to me. It was... I don't know, like the first time I ever connected with anyone.

The first time she ever connected with anyone.

We get older, we forget how it was being a teenager. Lost in our own heads, figuring out the world; we're the only ones going through these experiences.

You're always looking for that connection. It's why teenagers fall in love so easy. Why your parents always tell you to wait until you're older before you decide you really love someone.

Jesus, the first time she ever connected with anyone...

The tragedy of it all was that everyone who knew Mary seemed to think they connected with her. Or they knew her. Or they understood her.

But she felt disconnected from them. For all her popularity, all her intelligence, she just wanted to know who she was.

I supposed Deborah had offered her a chance to discover that.

I remember reading about how twins, separated at birth, can grow up apart and when they finally meet there's this intense spark. Like falling in love.

Is it the same with parents and their children? Just this sense of connection; an intense familiarity that breaks apart the whole world?

I skimmed through the transcript.

MARY: She was honest with me. Told me who she was. Said it had to be our secret.
DCI BRIGHT: You were coerced into –
MARY: I mean, no. I mean... She never made me do

anything I didn't want to do. Never forced me to feel anything for her. She wanted to protect me. You have to understand that.

I had to sit down. The transcript fell to the floor.

All Deborah Brown had ever wanted was to see her daughter. I got the feeling she had never asked the girl to accept her.

This woman who I had believed to be a psychopath. Unstable. Unhinged.

The number one rule of police work, the unwritten one. Not just on the Job but for life:

No one knows anything.

Everything is deceit and turnaround. Expectations count for shite.

I closed my eyes. Couldn't face reading any further.

Chapter 50

Another envelope came three days later.

Unmarked.

I opened the door, looked out into the close. Saw no one. Listened for the steps of someone further down.

Nothing.

I stepped back inside, opened the envelope.

A cheque.

From David Burns.

The amount would have set me up. Meant I could skip a few cases. Bought a holiday.

I held it up in front of the window, let the early morning sun that was threatening to melt the frost create a halo around the edges of the paper.

Then I tore it in two.

Kept going.

Let the shreds fall to the floor.

***

I opened the door, let Susan inside.

We kept our distance. Both afraid of something.

In the kitchen, the kettle boiling, she leaned on the worktop and looked me in the eye. Unwavering. "I'm on suspension."

"What?"

"A man died, McNee. All they have is our word that it was in self defence."

"Christ."

"They'll be asking you questions."

"Mary?"

"She's not saying anything about what happened in the cottage. All she'll say is that that bastard killed her mother. She claims the whole evening's a blur. The doctors say she has a concussion which could account for the memory loss. And maybe... maybe there are some things she'd simply rather try and forget."

I nodded. That made two of us.

The kettle boiled.

I almost thanked God. Gave me a chance to turn away from Susan. So she couldn't see. I blinked as I poured the water.

When I turned back round, she said, "This is a mess, right, Steed?"

I hesitated. Like I didn't know what she meant,

The here and now?

Or everything about us?

She reached out to me, placed her hand on top of mine.

I almost pulled away.

Almost.

Acknowledgements

Yes, there is no such paper as *The Dundee Herald*. And there's no such school as Bellview. Sometimes fiction writers have to invent stuff.

As ever, any errors in geography, continuity or any deviation from the real world are mine alone and made either through dramatic necessity or sheer stupidity on my part.

Anything that's right in the book, you can thank the following:

The guys behind the guy
Al "Sunshine" Guthrie: World's deadliest agent.
Ross Bradshaw: Scotman in exile, with some very sharp editorial suggestions.
John Schoenfelder: Taking McNee across the ocean in style.

The pushers
The cool kids at Waterstone's, Dundee; the old Blue Shirts (and Church) from the Flatman days; the rapscallions at Waterstone's, St Andrews; the crew

at Murder By the Book and, indeed, booksellers everywhere who deserve far more credit for the job they do.

The enablers
Jen Jordan; Jon Jordan; Ruth Jordan; Linda Landrigan; Sandra Ruttan; Tony Black; Steven Torres; Donna Moore; Charlie and Anne Marie Stella; Robert Simon MacDuff-Duncan; Jim Smith; Dave White; Kerry Shearer; Bob Mike and Christine from Beiderbeckes.

The back up
Rebecca Simpson; Gary Smith; Tim Stephen; Jennifer McDowall; Steven Wicks; Karen "Civilian Ambulance" Whyte; Renate Hutton; Lesley Nimmo.

The family
Dot and Martin McLean, my mum and dad, as ever.

And of course, readers everywhere. Even the ones who don't like bad language...